DATE DUE

AG 26 08	OCT 0 9 2015	
SE 19 08	JAN 2 9 2016	
MR 09 09	AUG 0 6 2016	
AG 19 09	AUG 0 5 2016	
MY 17 10		
MAY 2 6 2011		
IV 05 11		
AG 11 11		
Y 0 3 2012		
MAR 2 5 2013		
MAR 2 5 2013		
NOV 2 9 2013		
MAR 1 2 2014		
JAN 0 3 2014		
JUL 1 1 2015		
SEP 0 1 2015		
NOV 1 1 2015		

Demco, Inc. 38-293

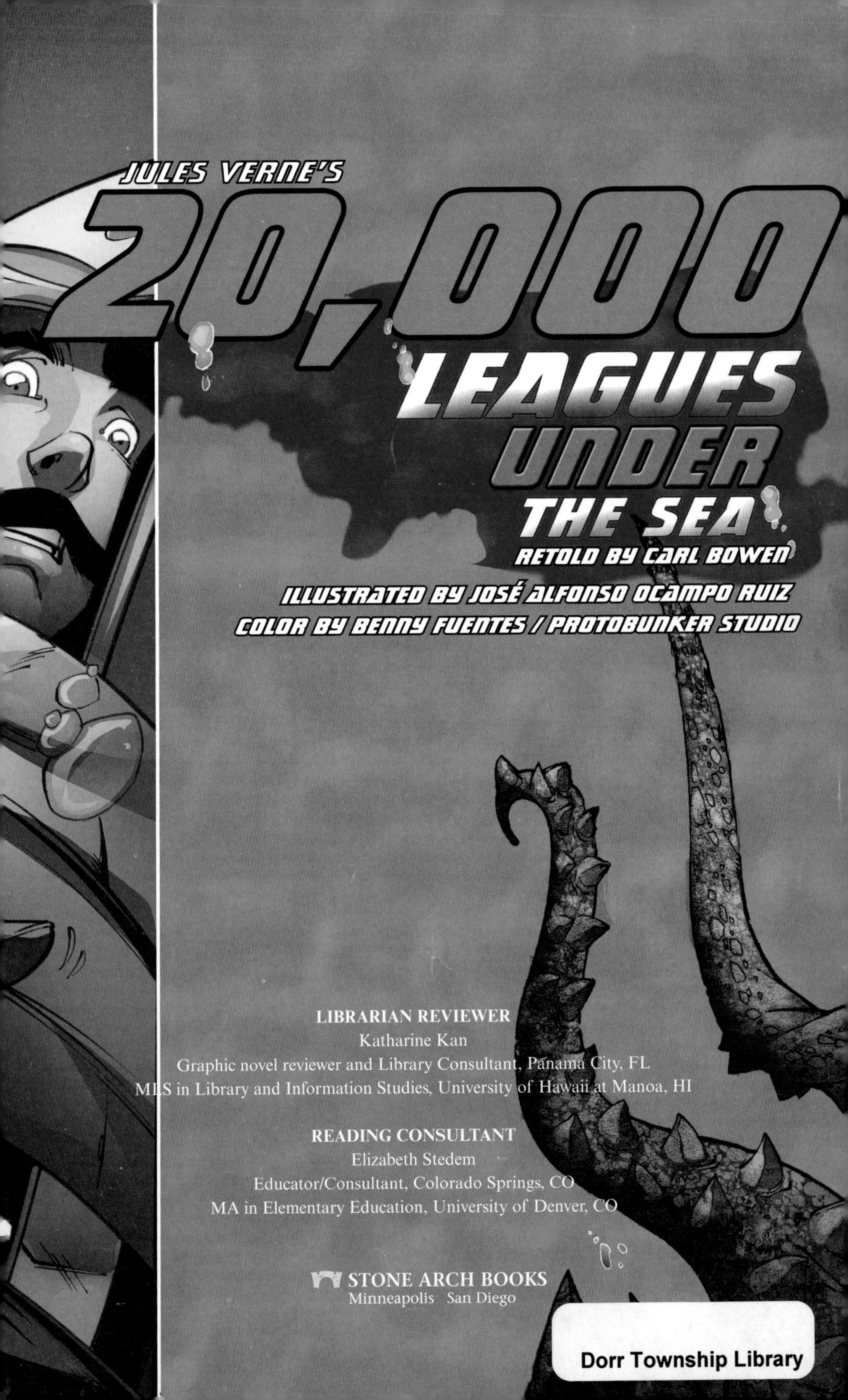

JULES VERNE'S

20,000 LEAGUES UNDER THE SEA

RETOLD BY CARL BOWEN

ILLUSTRATED BY JOSÉ ALFONSO OCAMPO RUIZ

COLOR BY BENNY FUENTES / PROTOBUNKER STUDIO

LIBRARIAN REVIEWER

Katharine Kan

Graphic novel reviewer and Library Consultant, Panama City, FL

MLS in Library and Information Studies, University of Hawaii at Manoa, HI

READING CONSULTANT

Elizabeth Stedem

Educator/Consultant, Colorado Springs, CO

MA in Elementary Education, University of Denver, CO

STONE ARCH BOOKS
Minneapolis San Diego

Graphic Revolve is published by Stone Arch Books,
151 Good Counsel Drive, P.O. Box 669,
Mankato, Minnesota 56002.
www.stonearchbooks.com

Copyright © 2008 by Stone Arch Books

Library of Congress Cataloging-in-Publication Data
Bowen, Carl.
  20,000 Leagues Under the Sea / by Jules Verne (retold by Carl Bowen); illustrated
José Alfonso Ocampo Ruiz.
  p. cm. — (Graphic Revolve)
  ISBN 978-1-4342-0447-9 (library binding)
  ISBN 978-1-4342-0497-4 (paperback)
  1. Graphic novels. I. Ocampo Ruiz, José Alfonso. II. Verne, Jules, 1828–1905. Vingt
mille lieues sous les mers. English. III. Title.
PN6727.B683A17 2008
741.5'973—dc22   2007030804

Summary: Scientist Pierre Aronnax and his trusty servant set sail to hunt a sea monster.
With help from Ned Land, the world's greatest harpooner, the men soon discover that the
creature is really a high-tech submarine. To keep this secret from being revealed, the sub's
leader, Captain Nemo, takes the men hostage. Now, each man must decide whether to trust
Nemo or try to escape this underwater world.

Art Director: Heather Kindseth
Graphic Designer: Kay Fraser
Color by Benny Fuentes and Protobunker Studio

1 2 3 4 5 6 13 12 11 10 09 08

TABLE OF CONTENTS

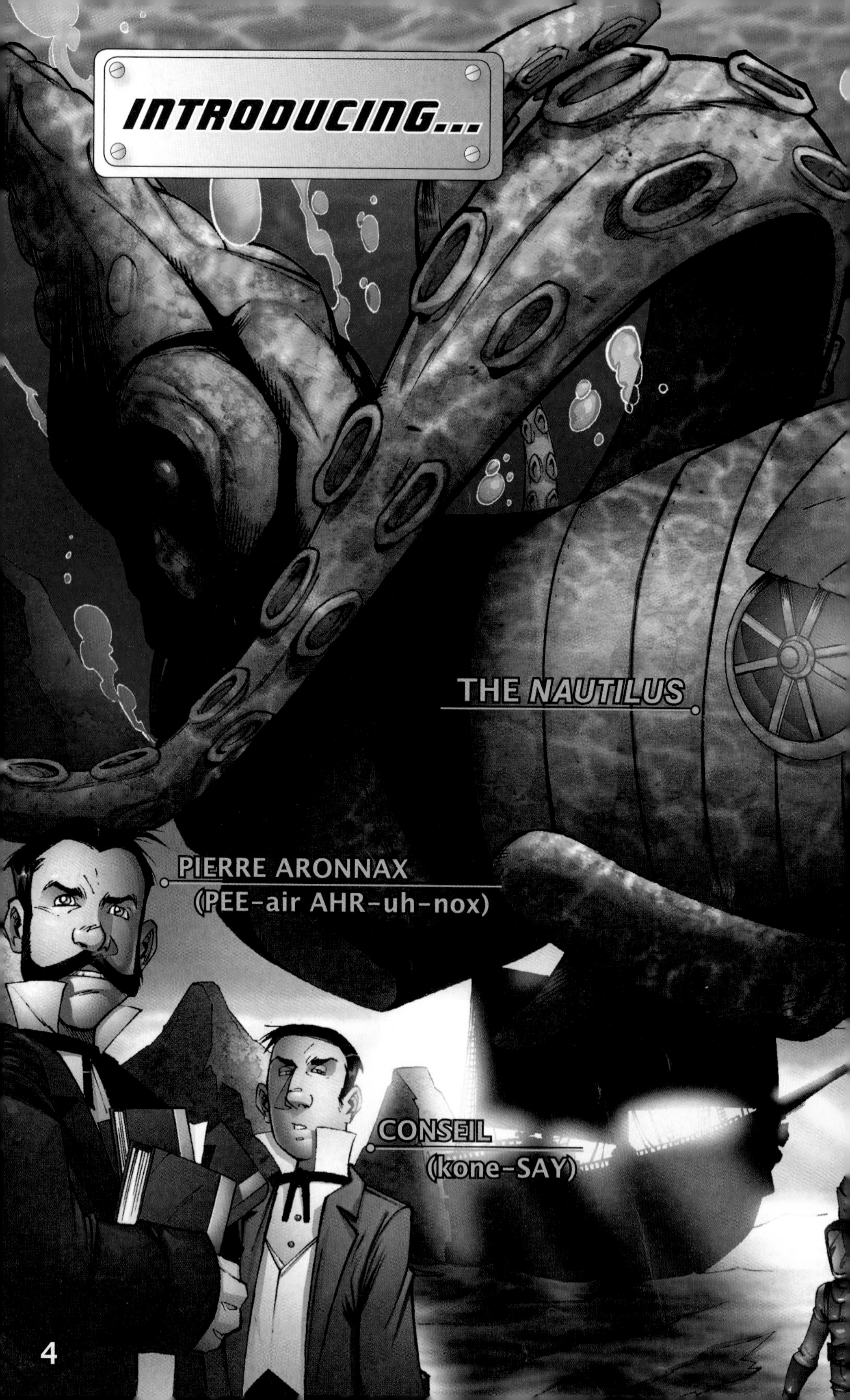
INTRODUCING...
THE NAUTILUS
PIERRE ARONNAX
(PEE-air AHR-uh-nox)
CONSEIL
(kone-SAY)

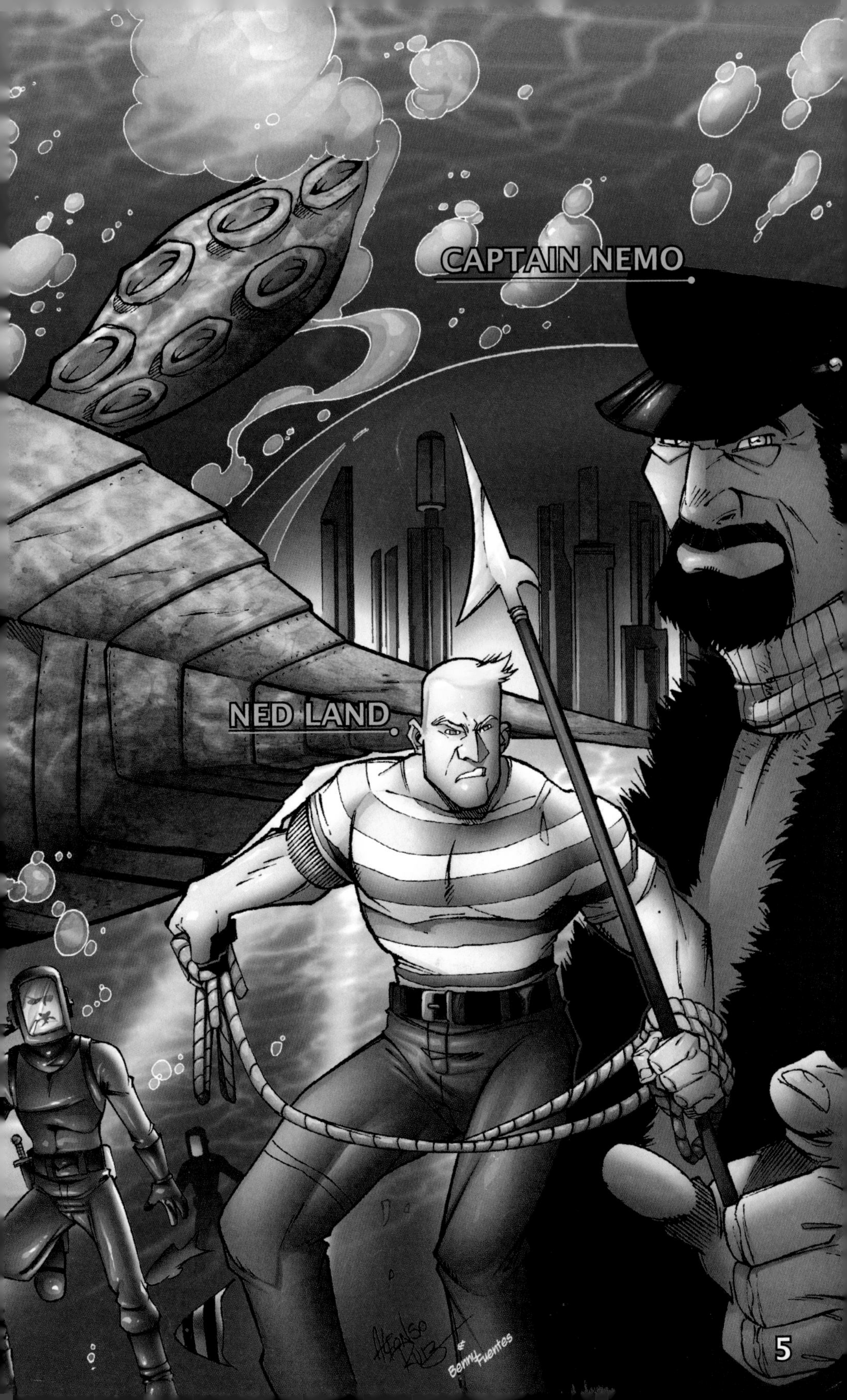
CAPTAIN NEMO
NED LAND

Chapter 1: The Hunt Begins

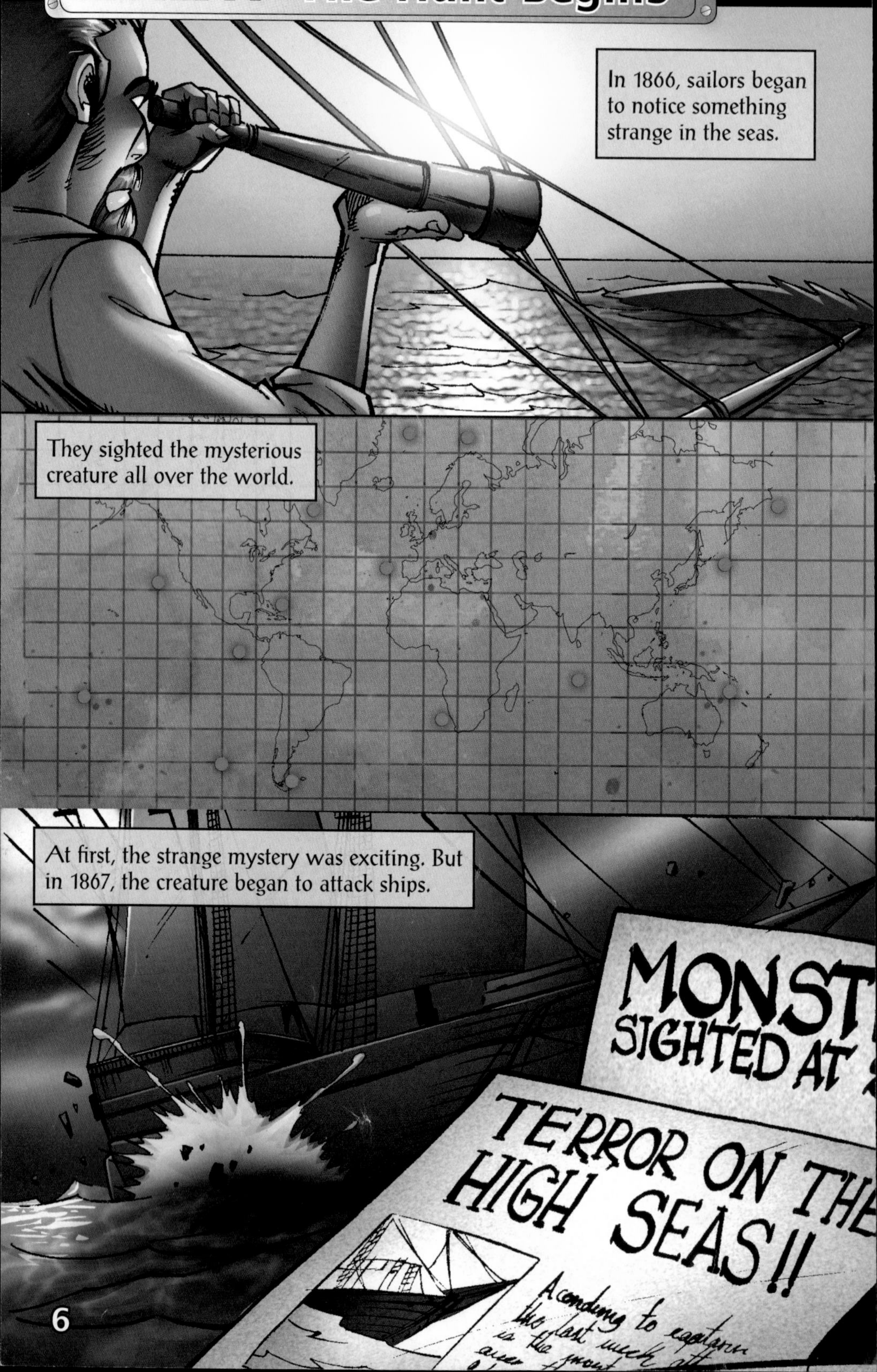

In 1866, sailors began to notice something strange in the seas.
They sighted the mysterious creature all over the world.
At first, the strange mystery was exciting. But in 1867, the creature began to attack ships.
MONST
SIGHTED AT
TERROR ON TH
HIGH SEAS!!

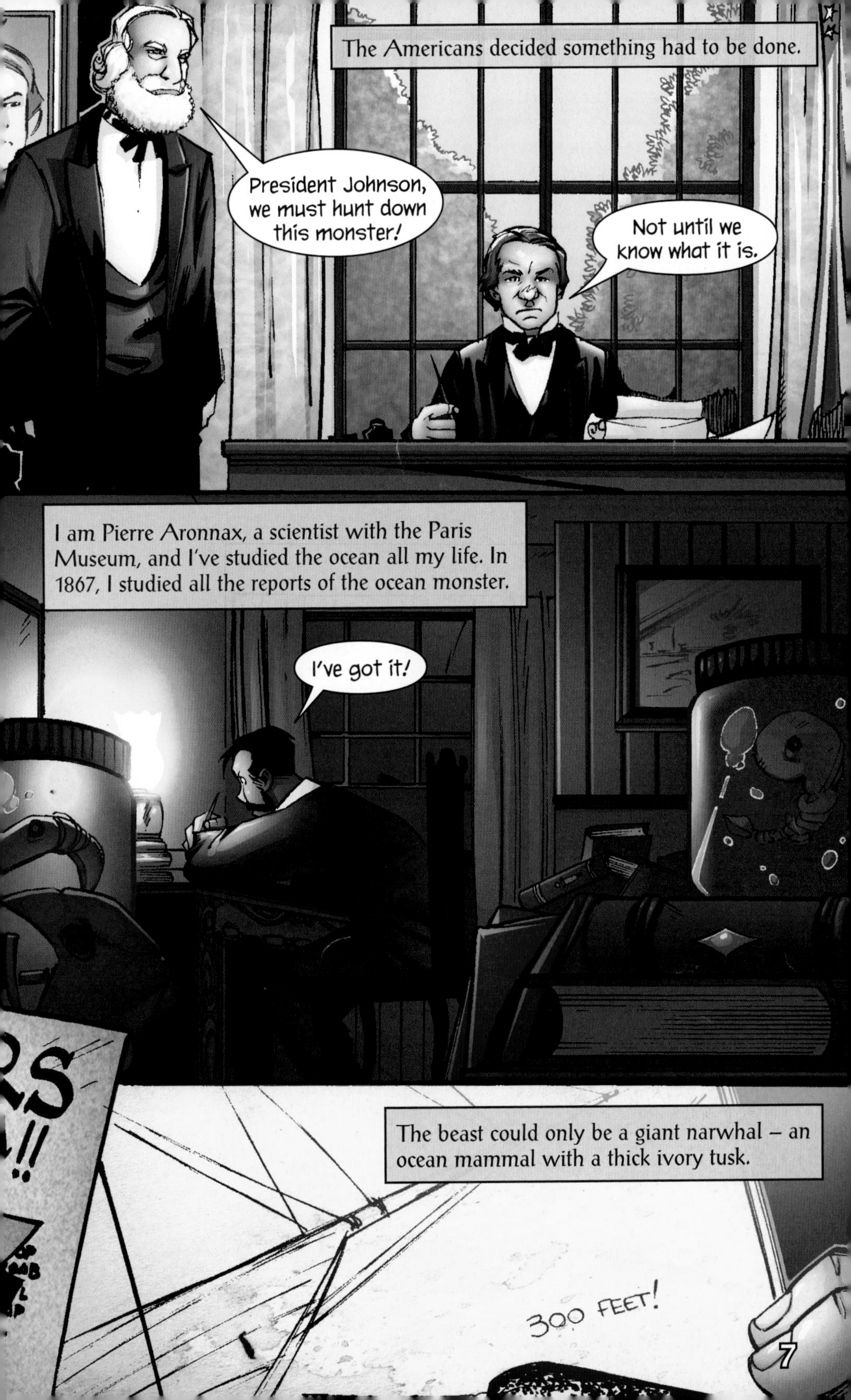
The Americans decided something had to be done.
President Johnson, we must hunt down this monster!
Not until we know what it is.
I am Pierre Aronnax, a scientist with the Paris Museum, and I've studied the ocean all my life. In 1867, I studied all the reports of the ocean monster.
I've got it!
The beast could only be a giant narwhal – an ocean mammal with a thick ivory tusk.
300 FEET!

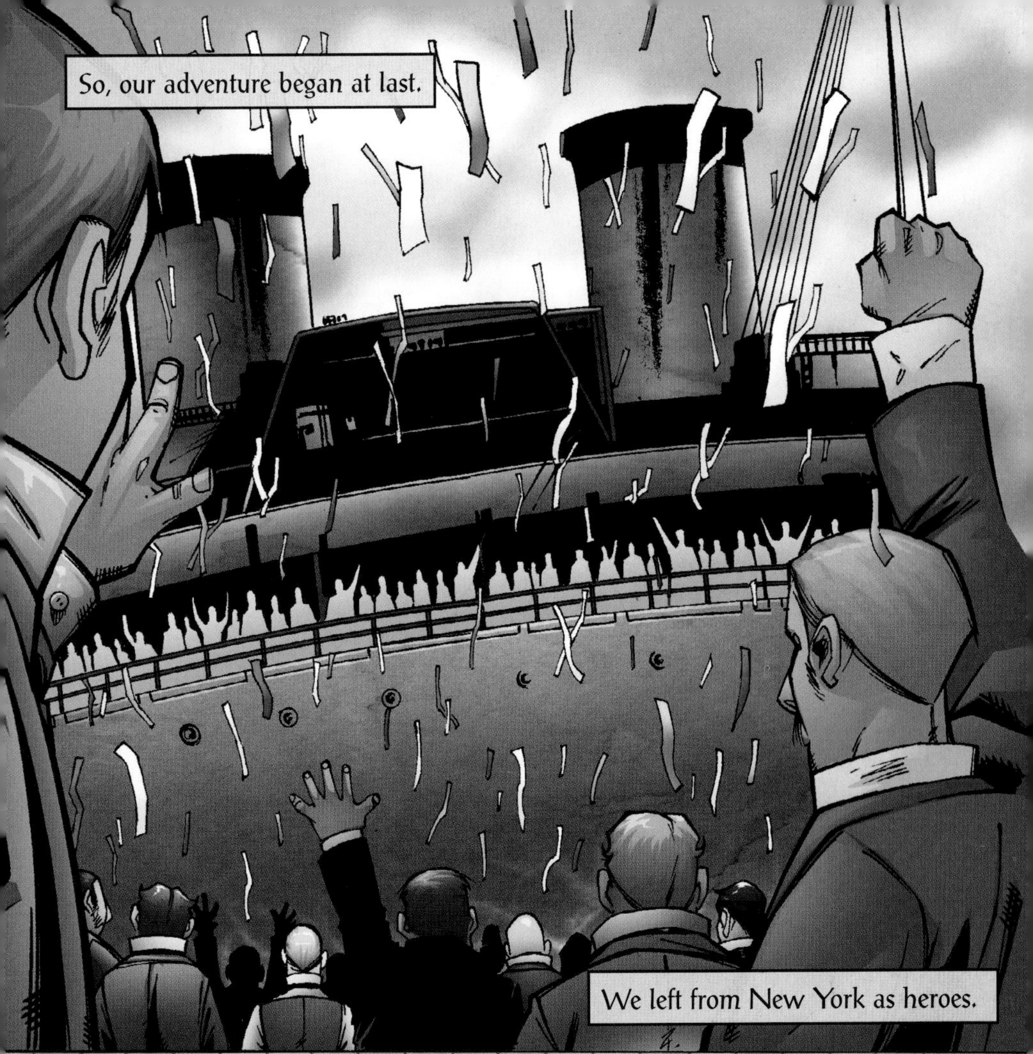
So, our adventure began at last.
We left from New York as heroes.

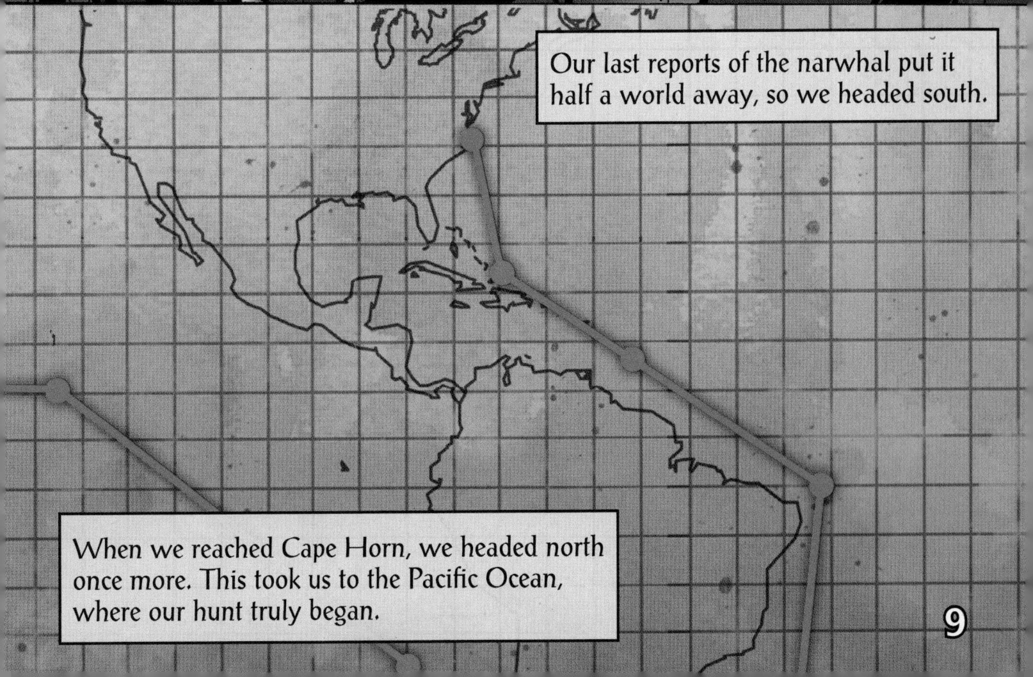
Our last reports of the narwhal put it half a world away, so we headed south.
When we reached Cape Horn, we headed north once more. This took us to the Pacific Ocean, where our hunt truly began.

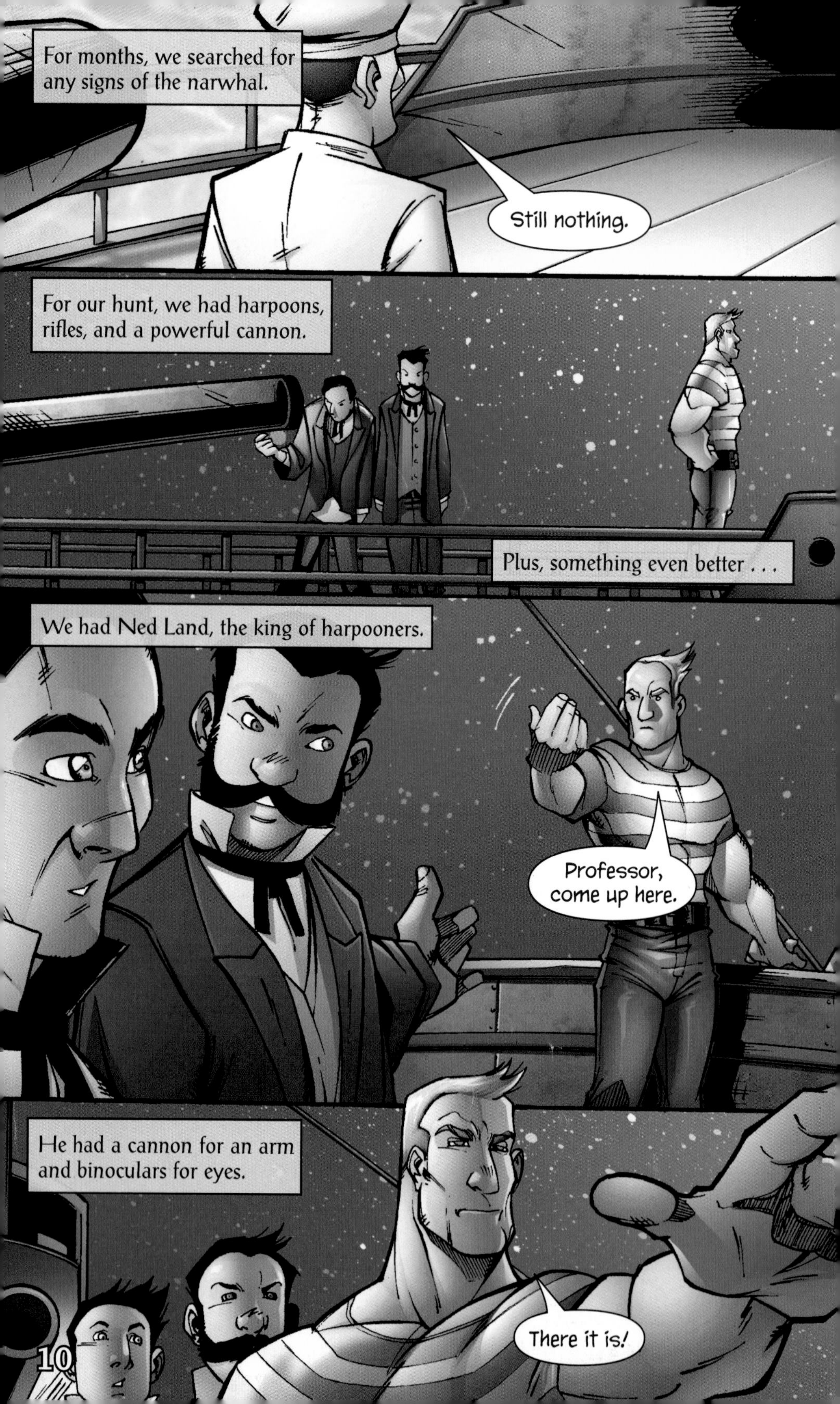
For months, we searched for any signs of the narwhal.
Still nothing.
For our hunt, we had harpoons, rifles, and a powerful cannon.
Plus, something even better . . .
We had Ned Land, the king of harpooners.
Professor, come up here.
He had a cannon for an arm and binoculars for eyes.
There it is!

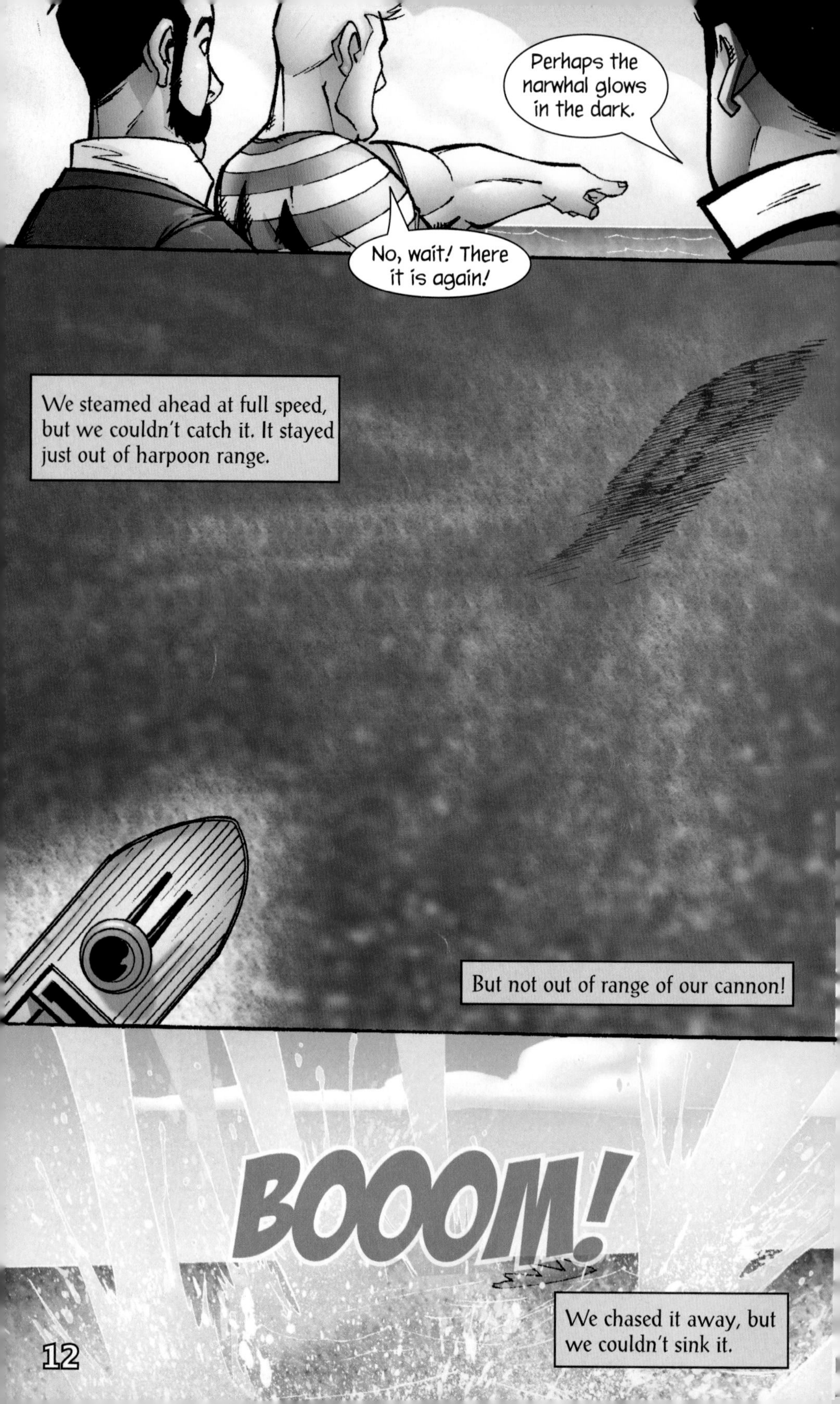
Perhaps the narwhal glows in the dark.
No, wait! There it is again!
We steamed ahead at full speed, but we couldn't catch it. It stayed just out of harpoon range.
But not out of range of our cannon!
BOOOM!
We chased it away, but we couldn't sink it.

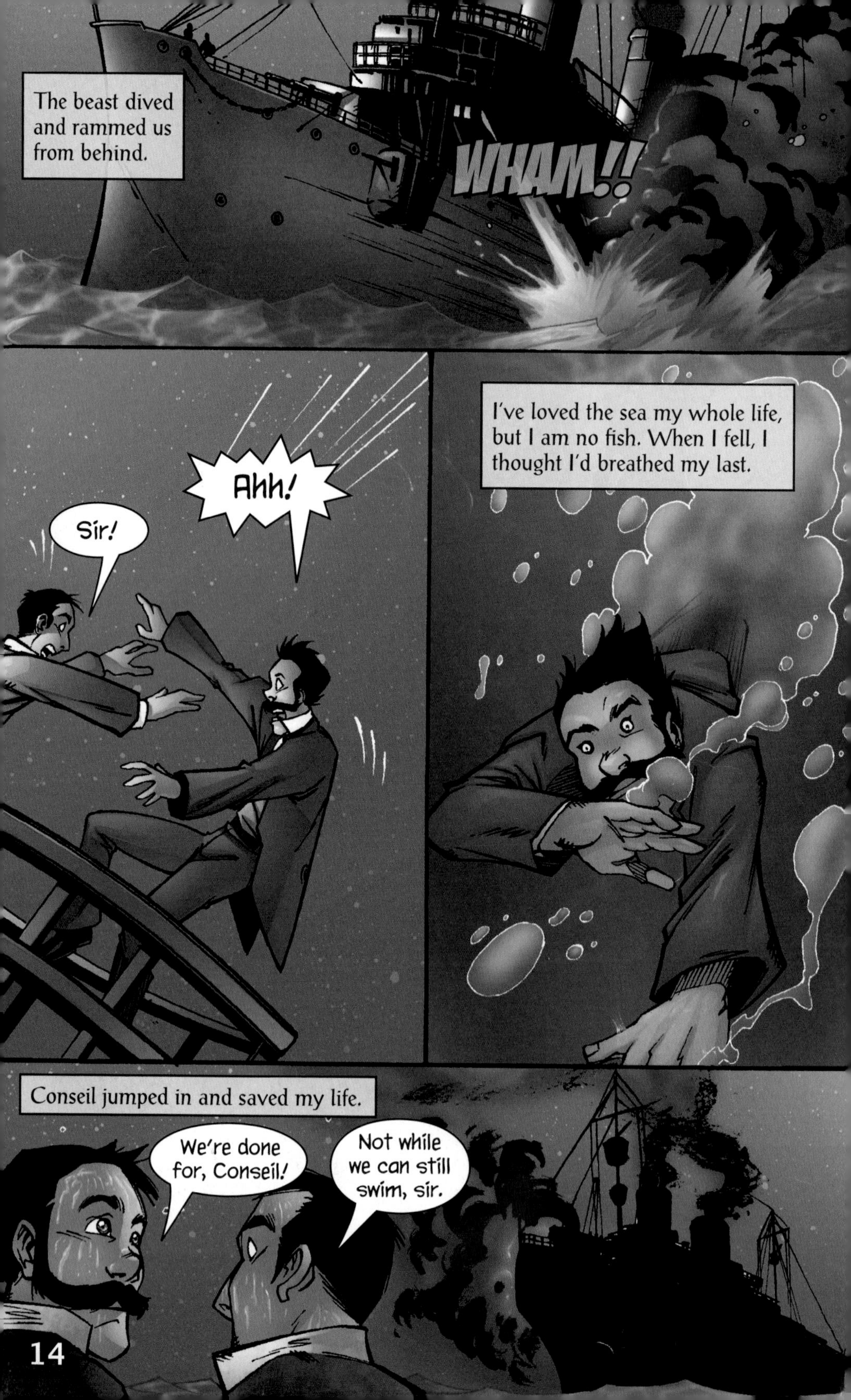
The beast dived and rammed us from behind.
WHAM!!
Sir!
Ahh!
I've loved the sea my whole life, but I am no fish. When I fell, I thought I'd breathed my last.
Conseil jumped in and saved my life.
We're done for, Conseil!
Not while we can still swim, sir.

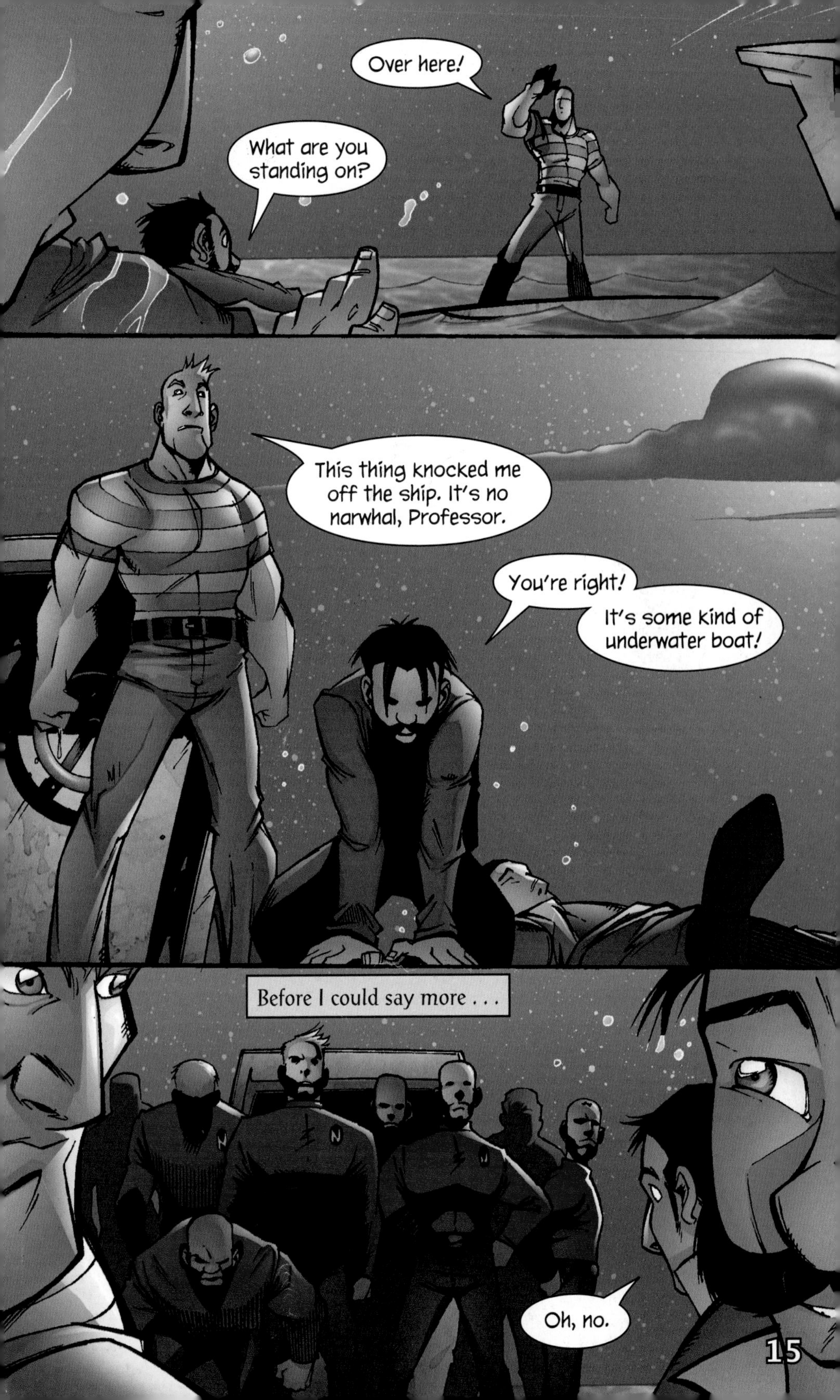
Over here!
What are you standing on?
This thing knocked me off the ship. It's no narwhal, Professor.
You're right!
It's some kind of underwater boat!
Before I could say more . . .
Oh, no.

CHAPTER 2: Inside the *Nautilus*

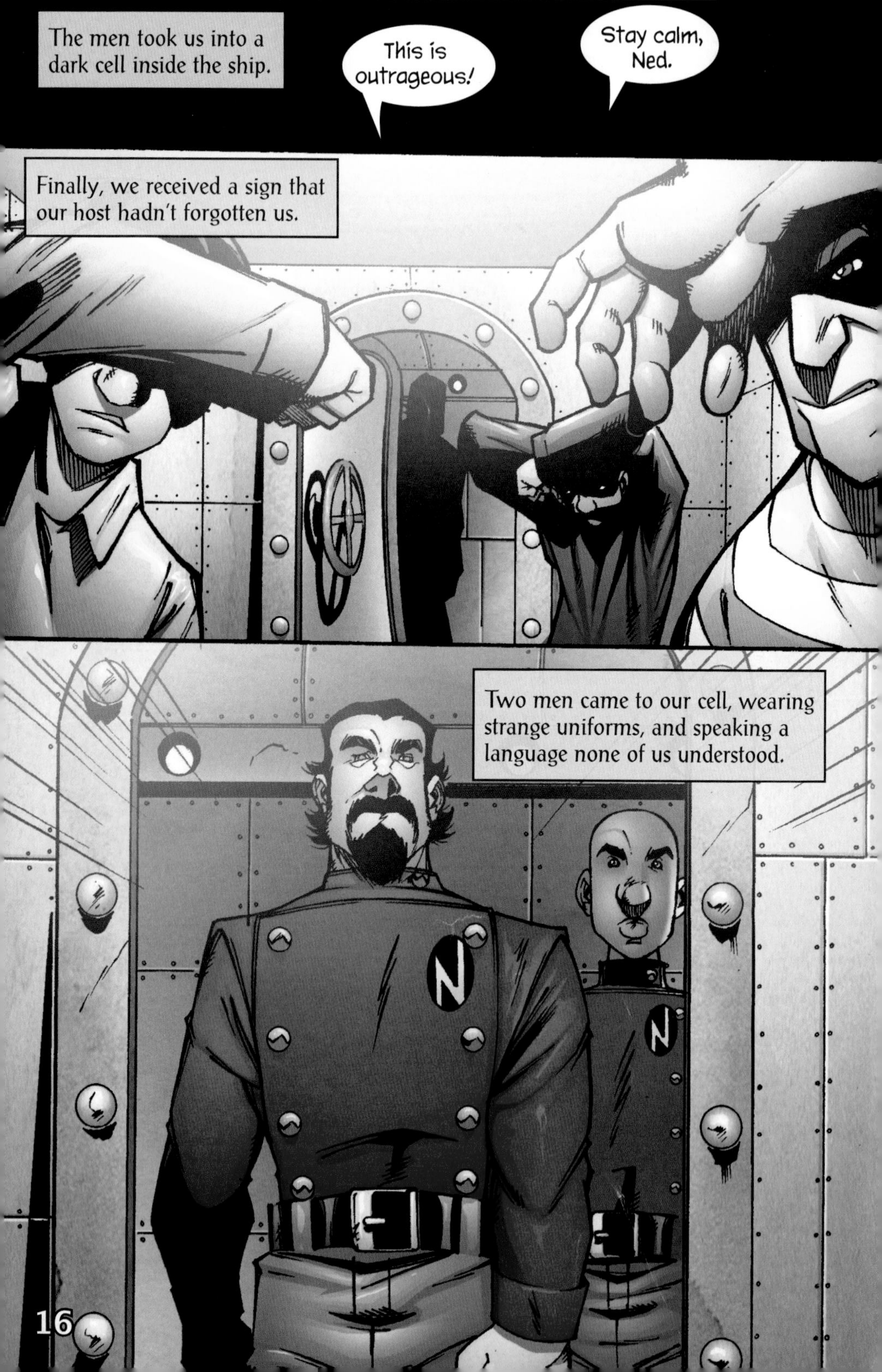
The men took us into a dark cell inside the ship.
This is outrageous!
Stay calm, Ned.
Finally, we received a sign that our host hadn't forgotten us.
Two men came to our cell, wearing strange uniforms, and speaking a language none of us understood.

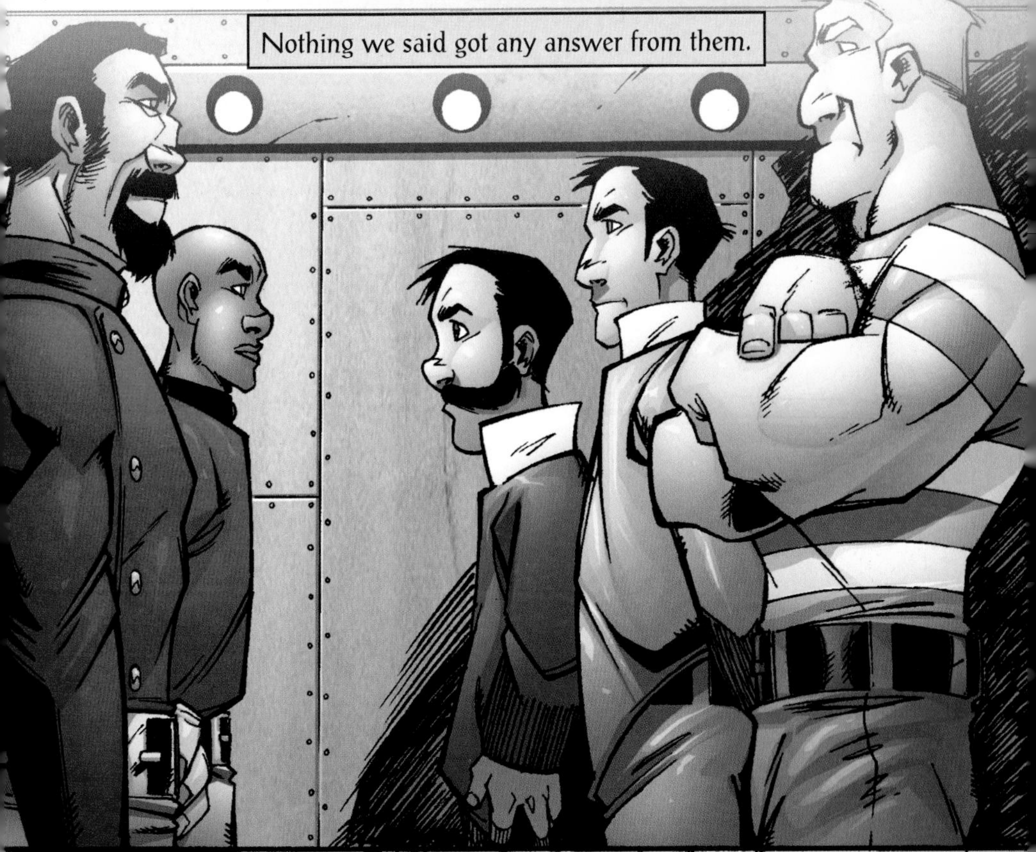
Nothing we said got any answer from them.

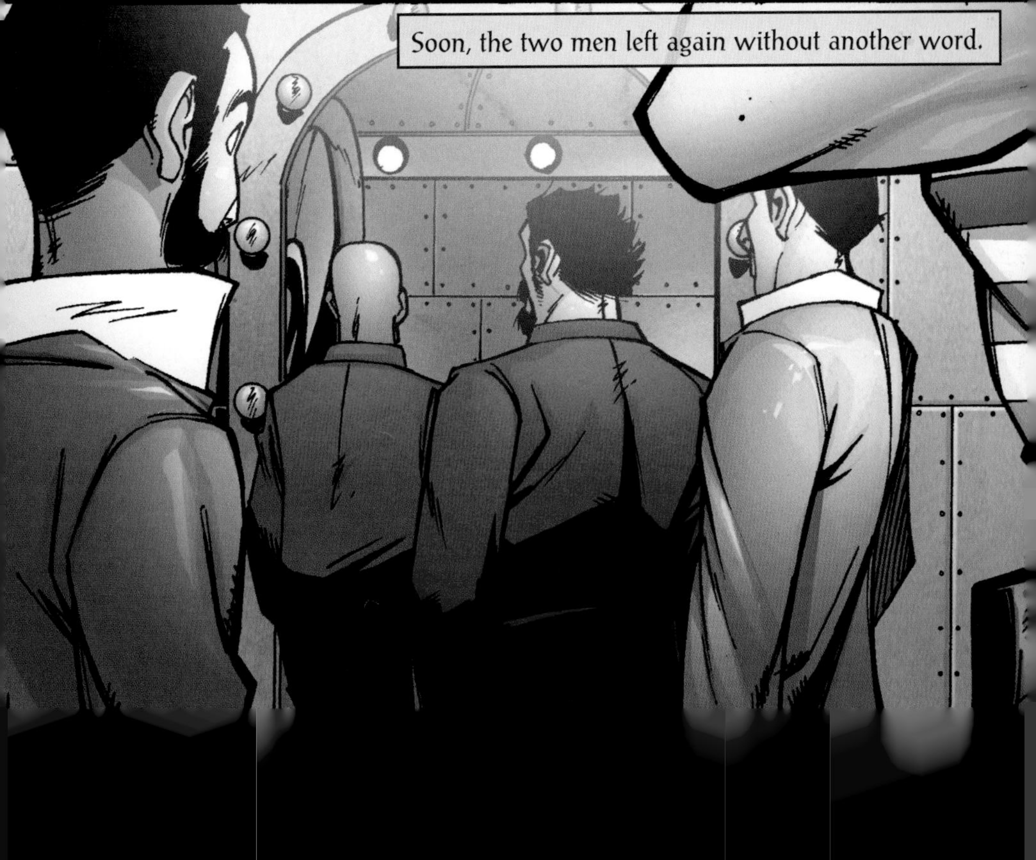
Soon, the two men left again without another word.

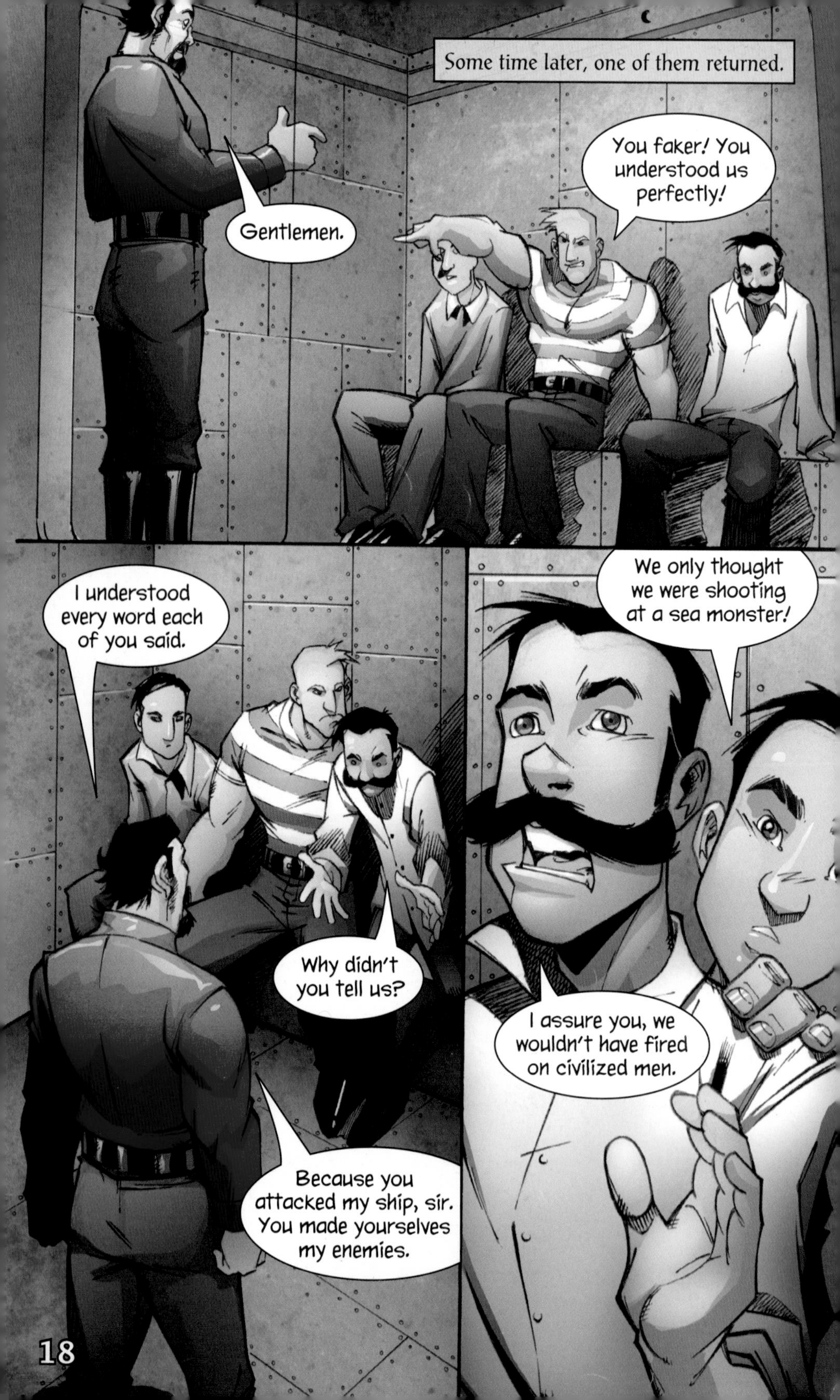
Some time later, one of them returned.
Gentlemen.
You faker! You understood us perfectly!
I understood every word each of you said.
Why didn't you tell us?
Because you attacked my ship, sir. You made yourselves my enemies.
We only thought we were shooting at a sea monster!
I assure you, we wouldn't have fired on civilized men.

After that, our host offered us dinner and a tour.

Ned and Conseil wanted to eat first, but I wanted to see the ship.

Our host showed me his favorite rooms, including the engine room and his library.

Then he showed me the lounge at the front of the ship.

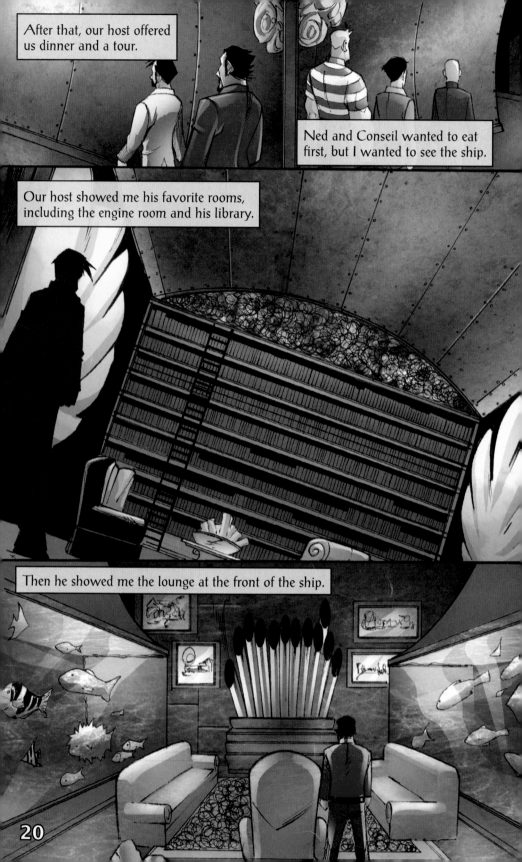

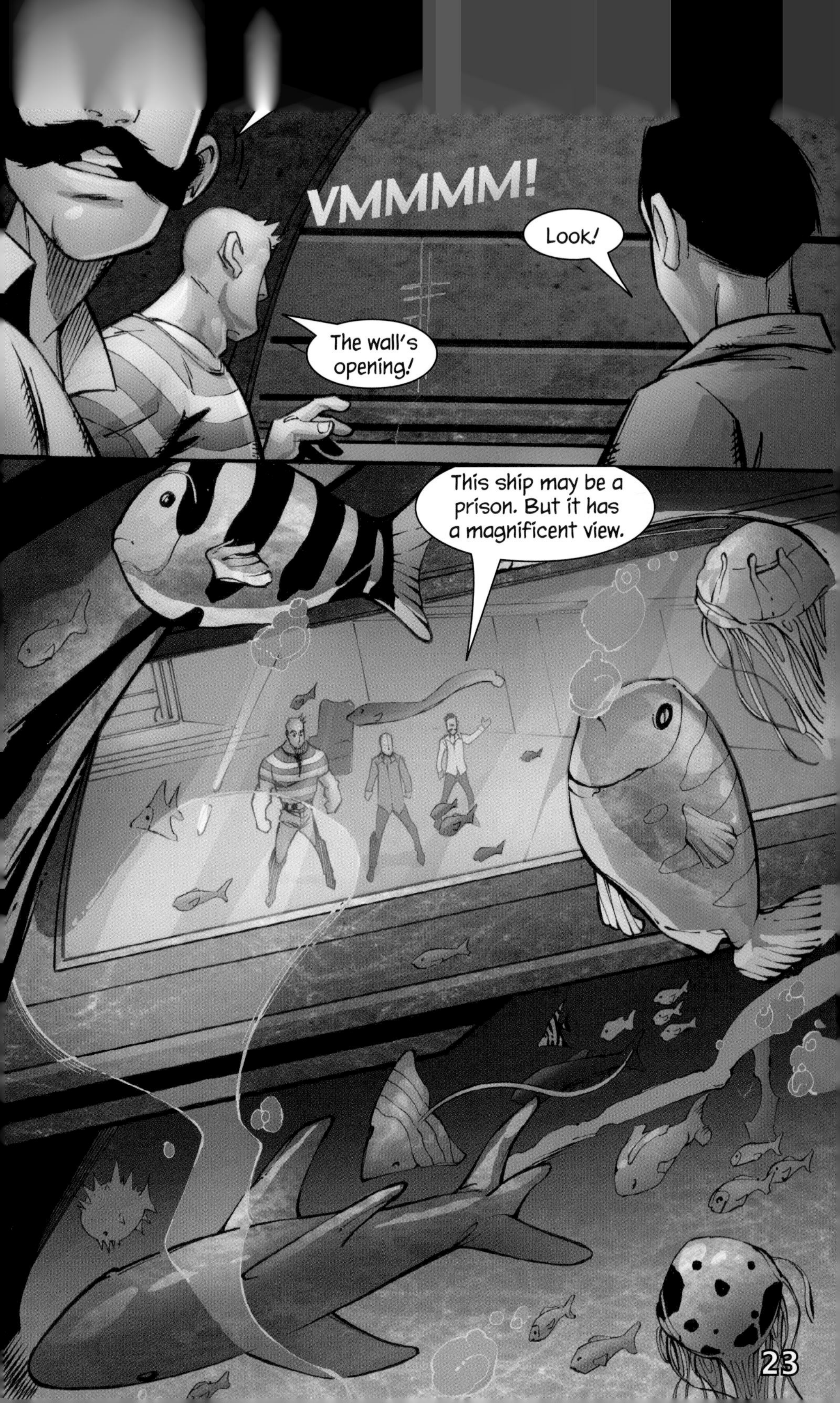
VMMMM!
Look!
The wall's opening!
This ship may be a prison. But it has a magnificent view.

CHAPTER 3 : Death at Sea

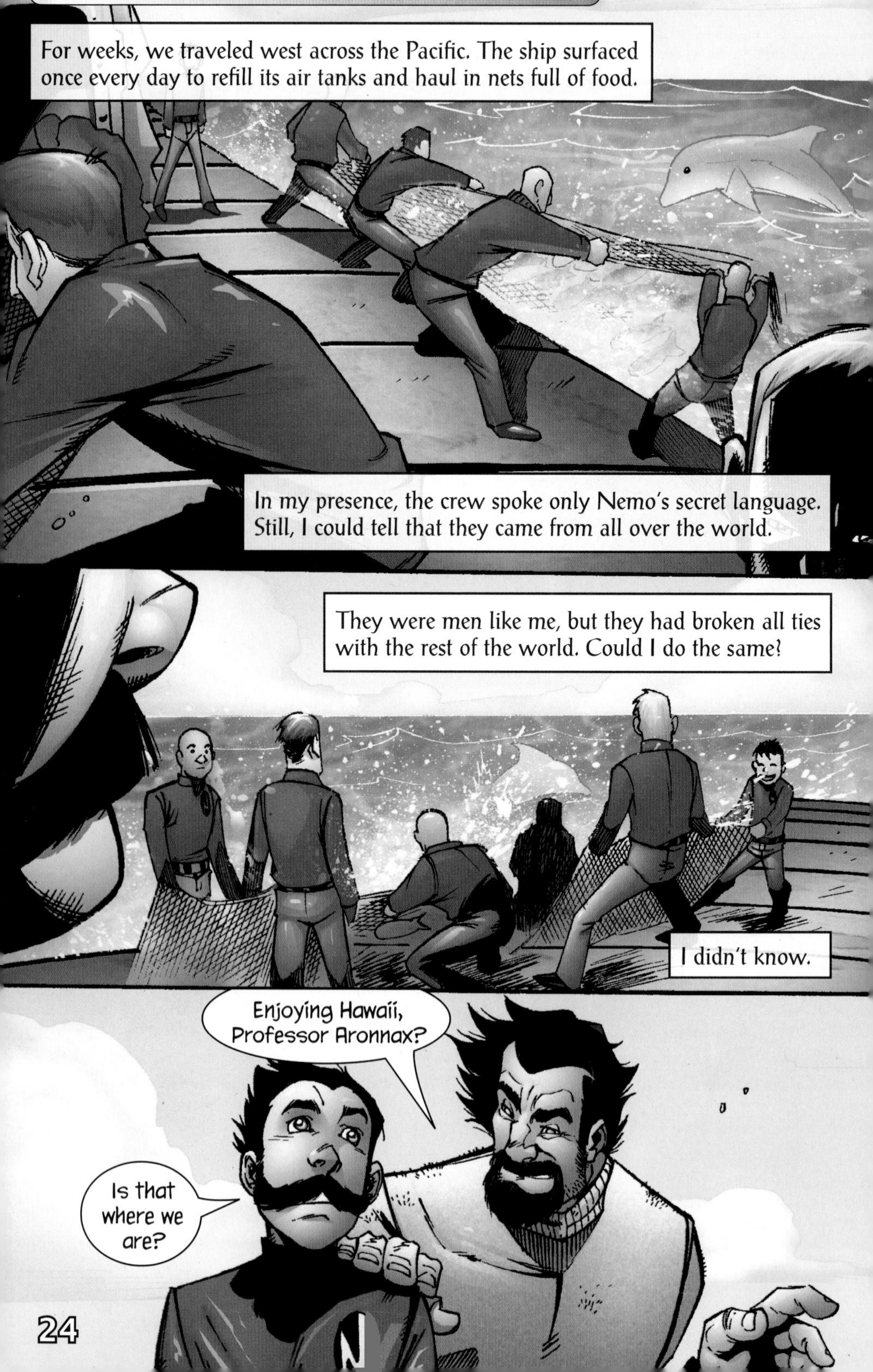

For weeks, we traveled west across the Pacific. The ship surfaced once every day to refill its air tanks and haul in nets full of food.
In my presence, the crew spoke only Nemo's secret language. Still, I could tell that they came from all over the world.
They were men like me, but they had broken all ties with the rest of the world. Could I do the same?
I didn't know.
Enjoying Hawaii, Professor Aronnax?
Is that where we are?

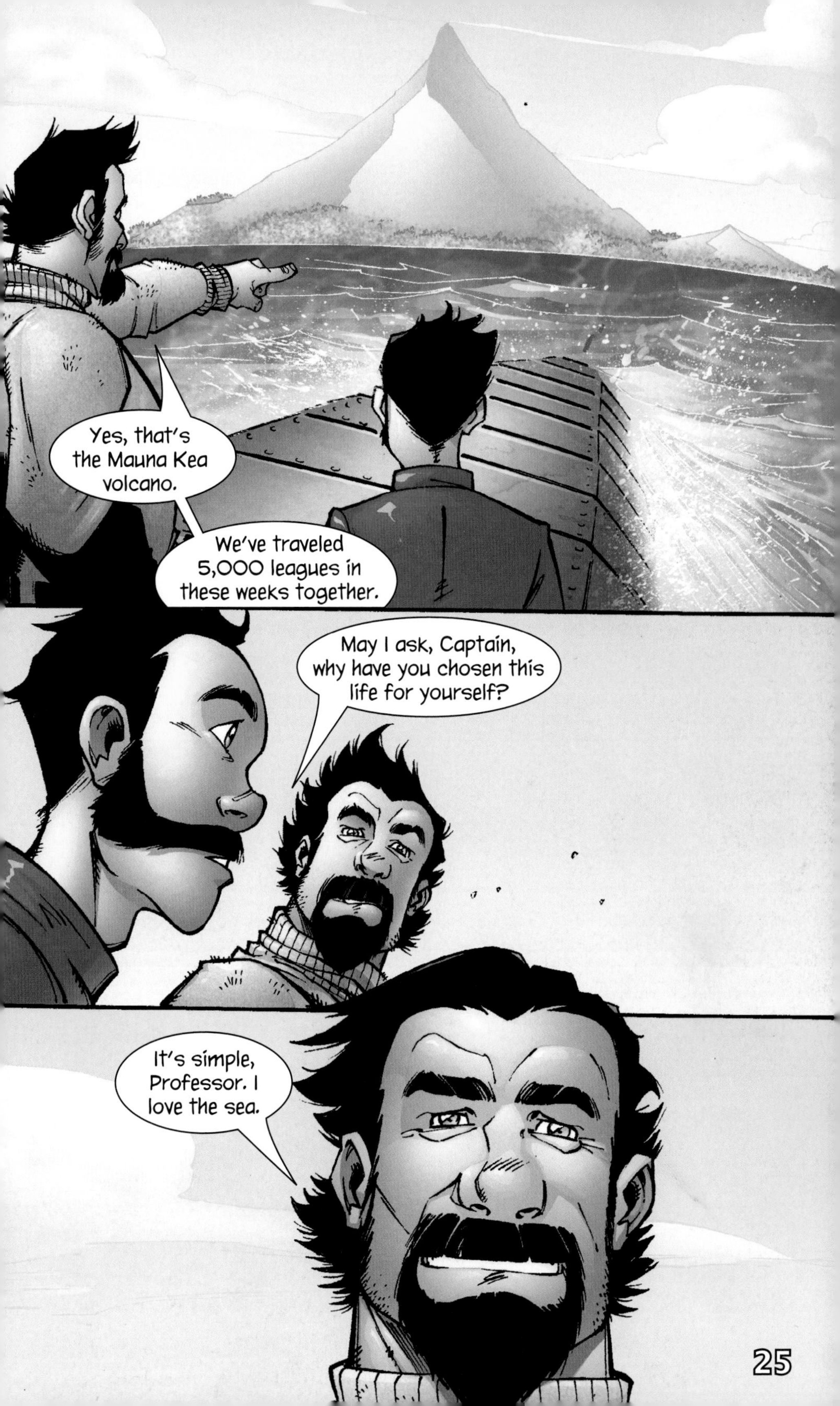

Yes, that's the Mauna Kea volcano.
We've traveled 5,000 leagues in these weeks together.
May I ask, Captain, why have you chosen this life for yourself?
It's simple, Professor. I love the sea.

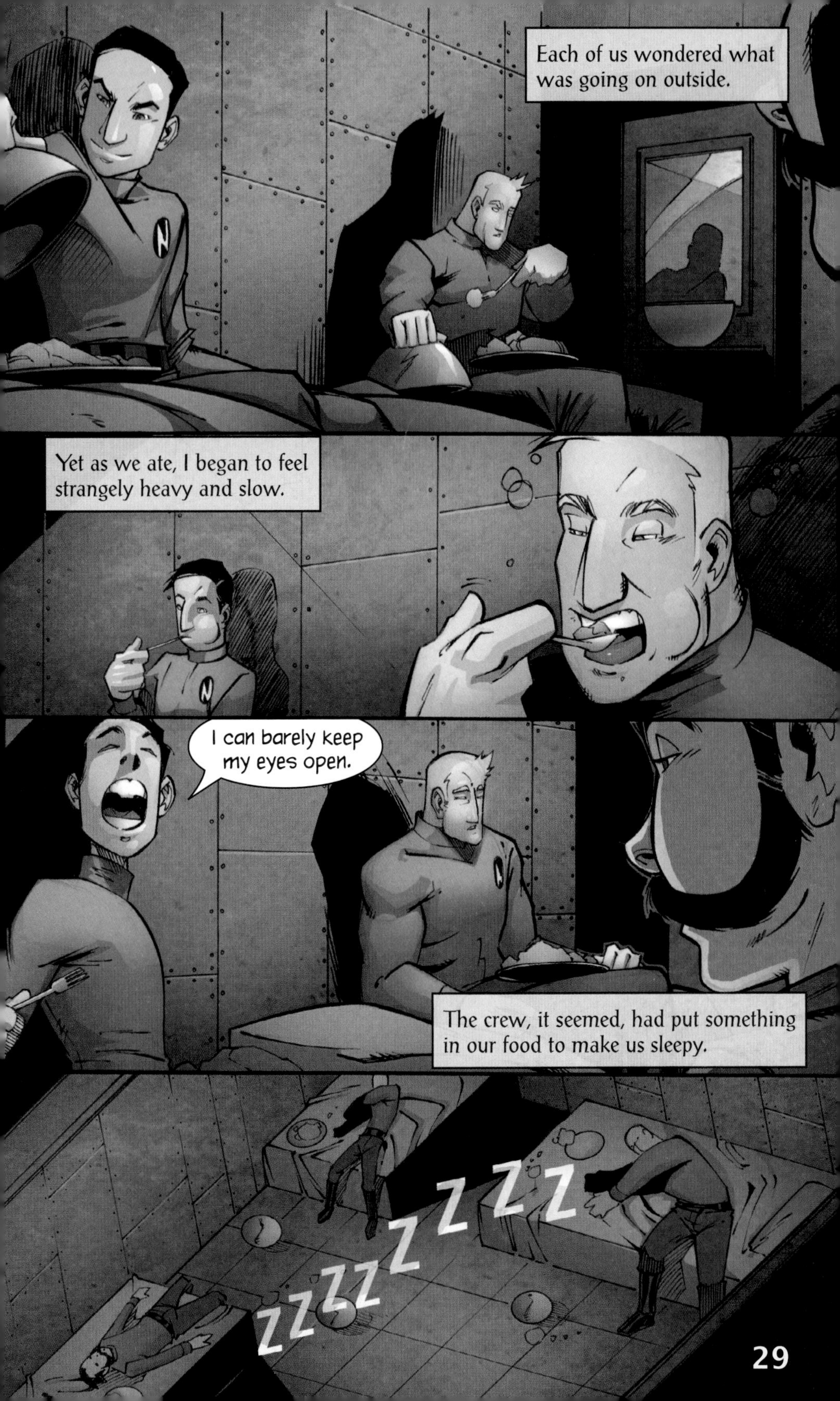
Each of us wondered what was going on outside.
Yet as we ate, I began to feel strangely heavy and slow.
I can barely keep my eyes open.
The crew, it seemed, had put something in our food to make us sleepy.
ZZZZZZZZZ

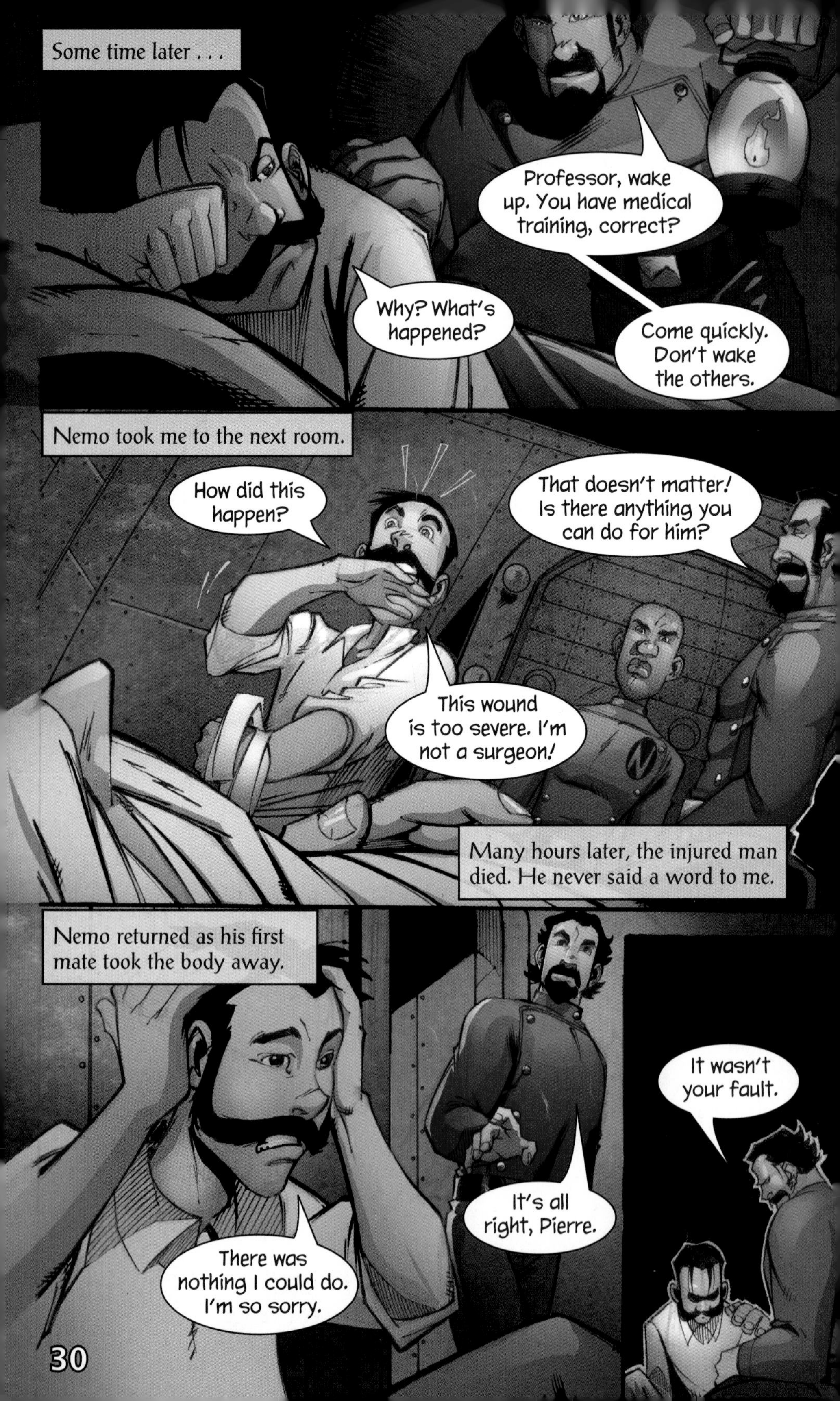
Some time later . . .
Professor, wake up. You have medical training, correct?
Why? What's happened?
Come quickly. Don't wake the others.
Nemo took me to the next room.
How did this happen?
That doesn't matter! Is there anything you can do for him?
This wound is too severe. I'm not a surgeon!
Many hours later, the injured man died. He never said a word to me.
Nemo returned as his first mate took the body away.
It wasn't your fault.
It's all right, Pierre.
There was nothing I could do. I'm so sorry.

CHAPTER 4 : Underwater Adventures

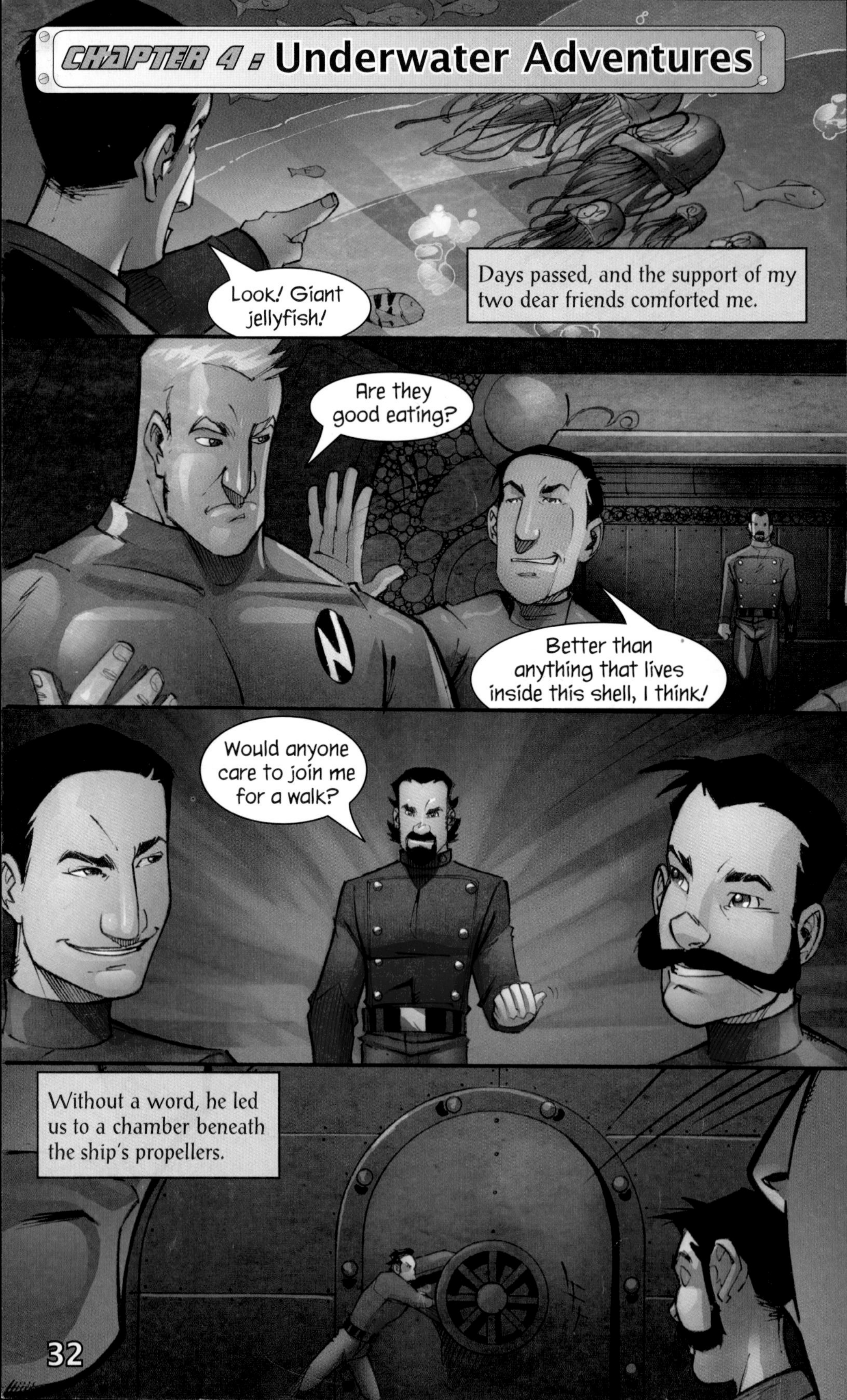
Look! Giant jellyfish!
Days passed, and the support of my two dear friends comforted me.
Are they good eating?
Better than anything that lives inside this shell, I think!
Would anyone care to join me for a walk?
Without a word, he led us to a chamber beneath the ship's propellers.

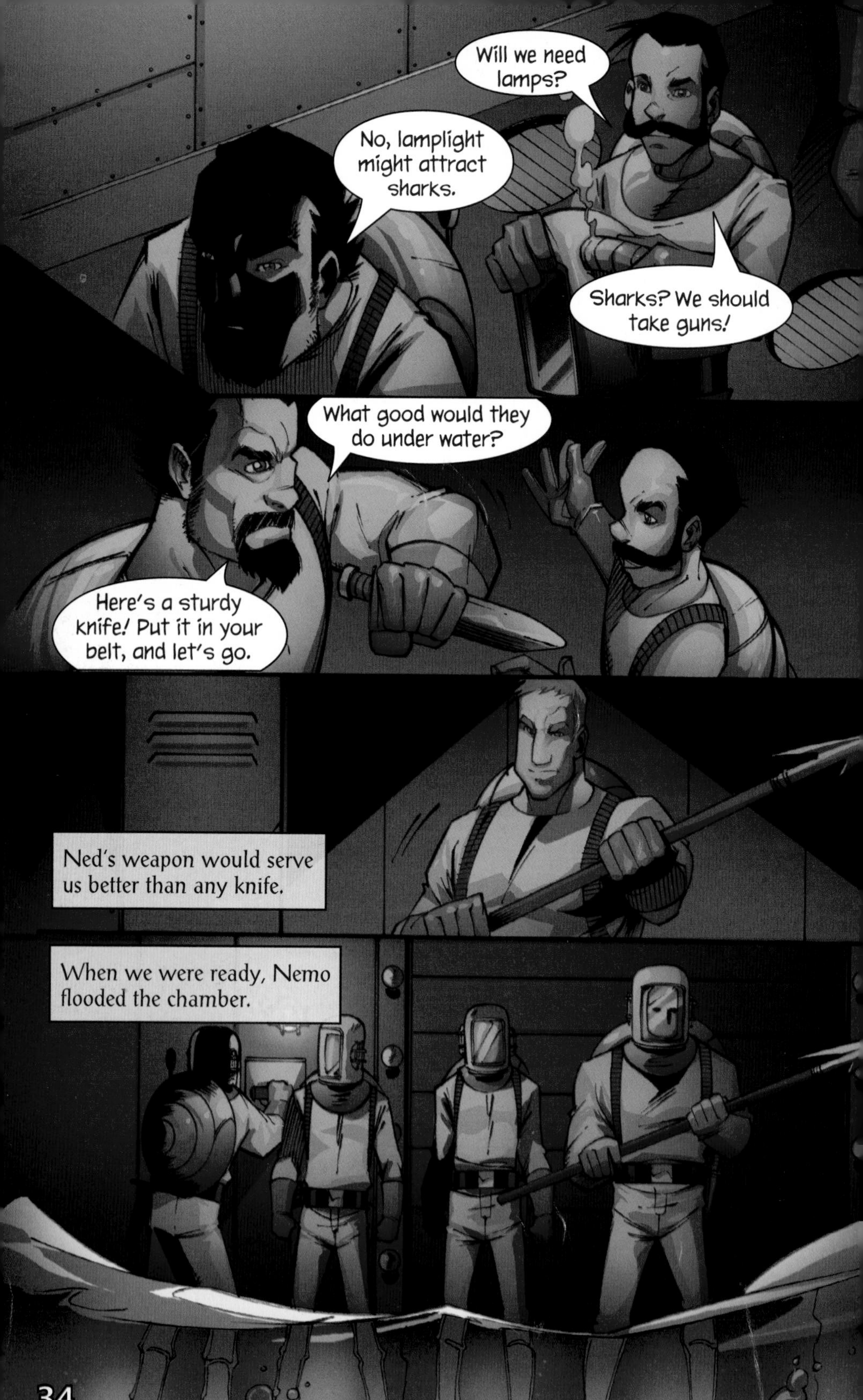
Will we need lamps?
No, lamplight might attract sharks.
Sharks? We should take guns!
What good would they do under water?
Here's a sturdy knife! Put it in your belt, and let's go.
Ned's weapon would serve us better than any knife.
When we were ready, Nemo flooded the chamber.

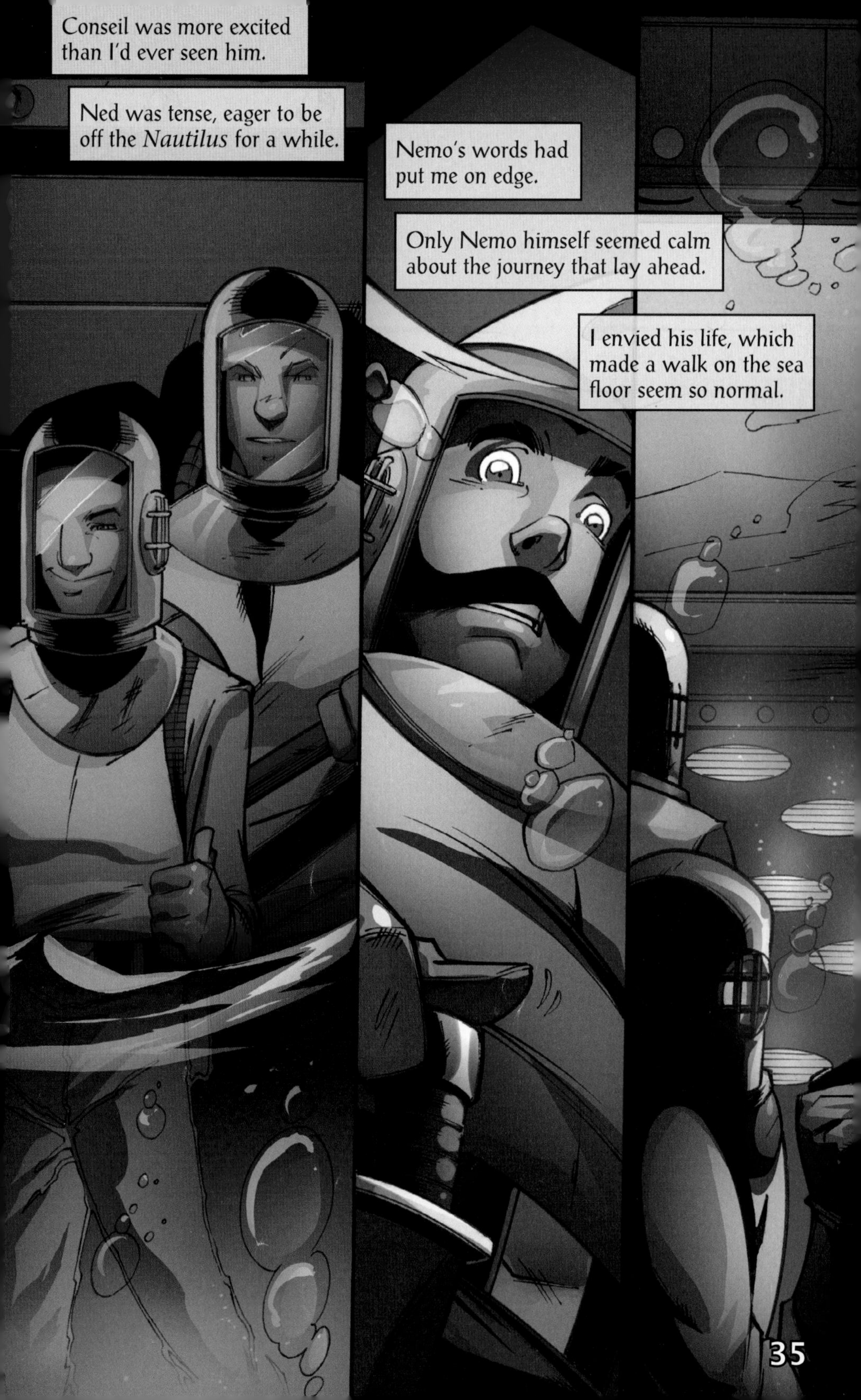
Conseil was more excited than I'd ever seen him.
Ned was tense, eager to be off the *Nautilus* for a while.
Nemo's words had put me on edge.
Only Nemo himself seemed calm about the journey that lay ahead.
I envied his life, which made a walk on the sea floor seem so normal.

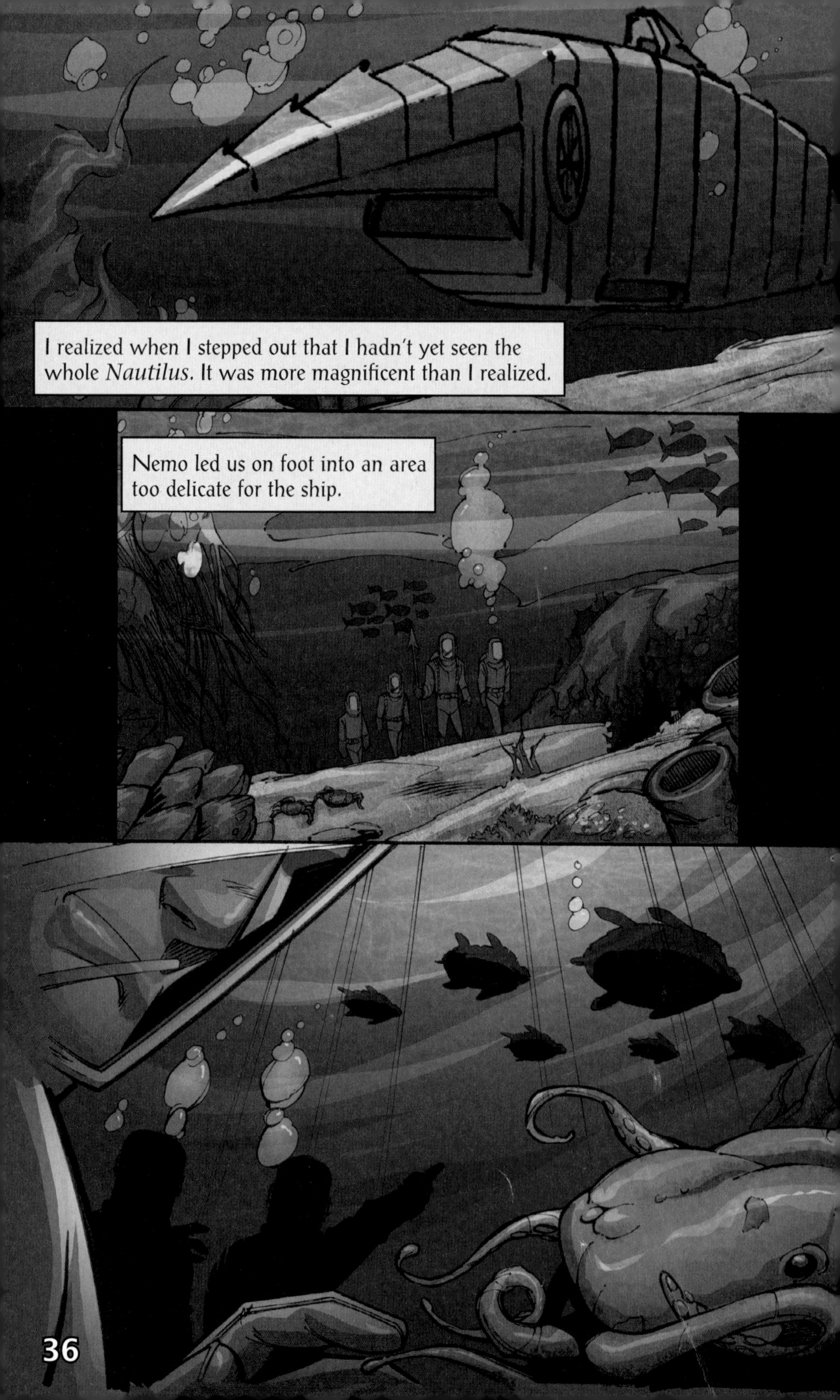
I realized when I stepped out that I hadn't yet seen the whole *Nautilus*. It was more magnificent than I realized.
Nemo led us on foot into an area too delicate for the ship.

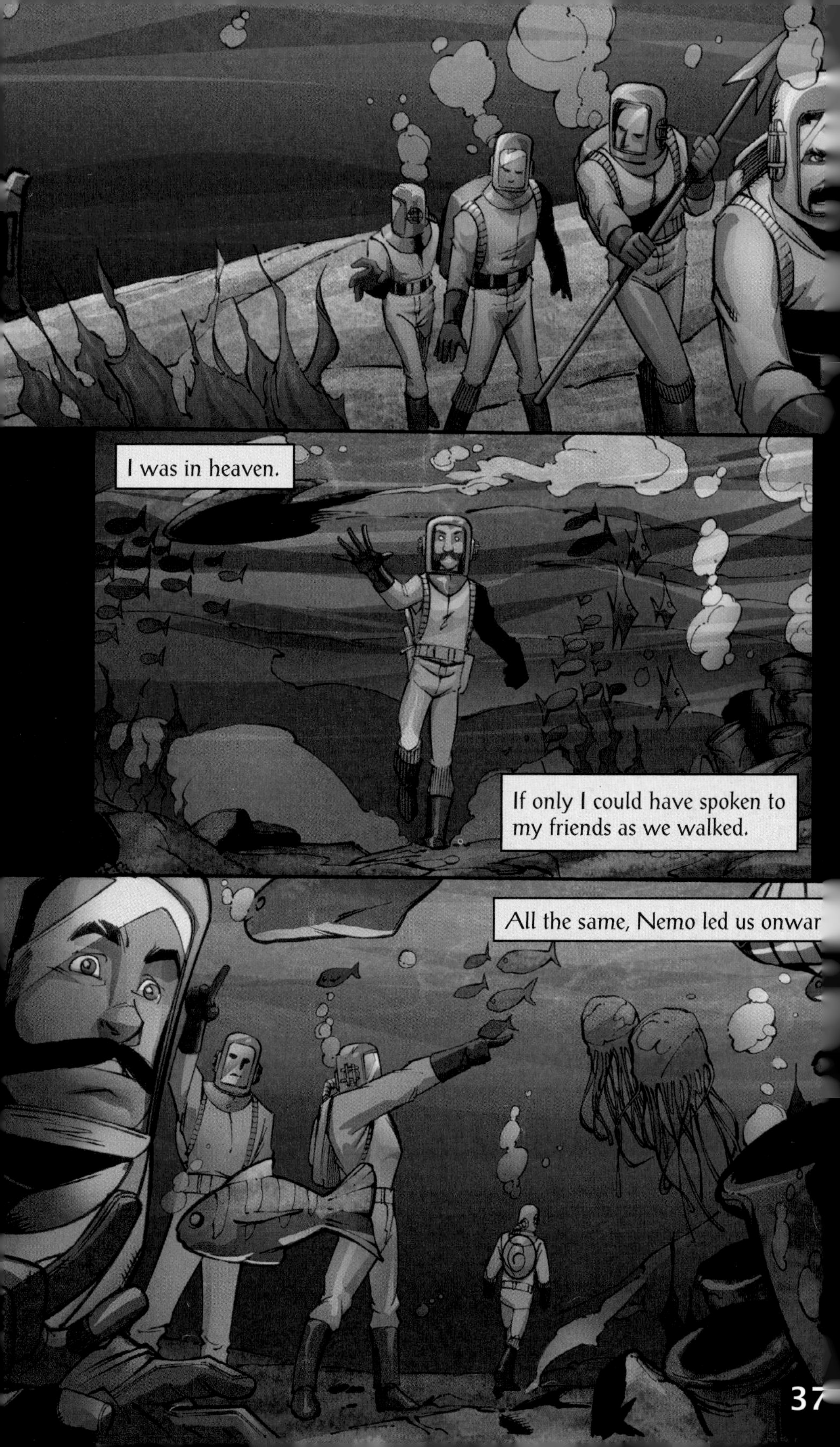
I was in heaven.
If only I could have spoken to my friends as we walked.
All the same, Nemo led us onwar

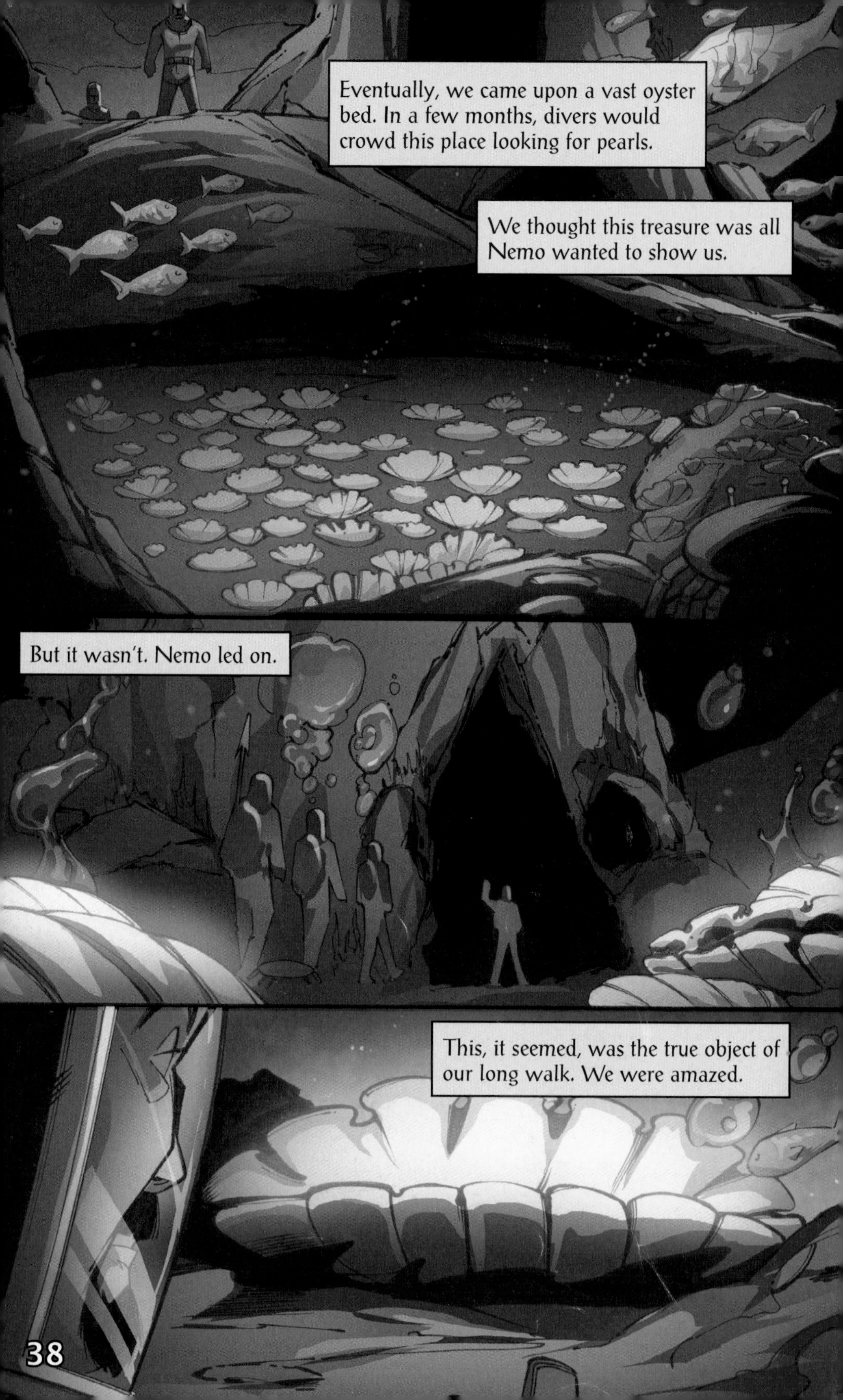
Eventually, we came upon a vast oyster bed. In a few months, divers would crowd this place looking for pearls.
We thought this treasure was all Nemo wanted to show us.
But it wasn't. Nemo led on.
This, it seemed, was the true object of our long walk. We were amazed.

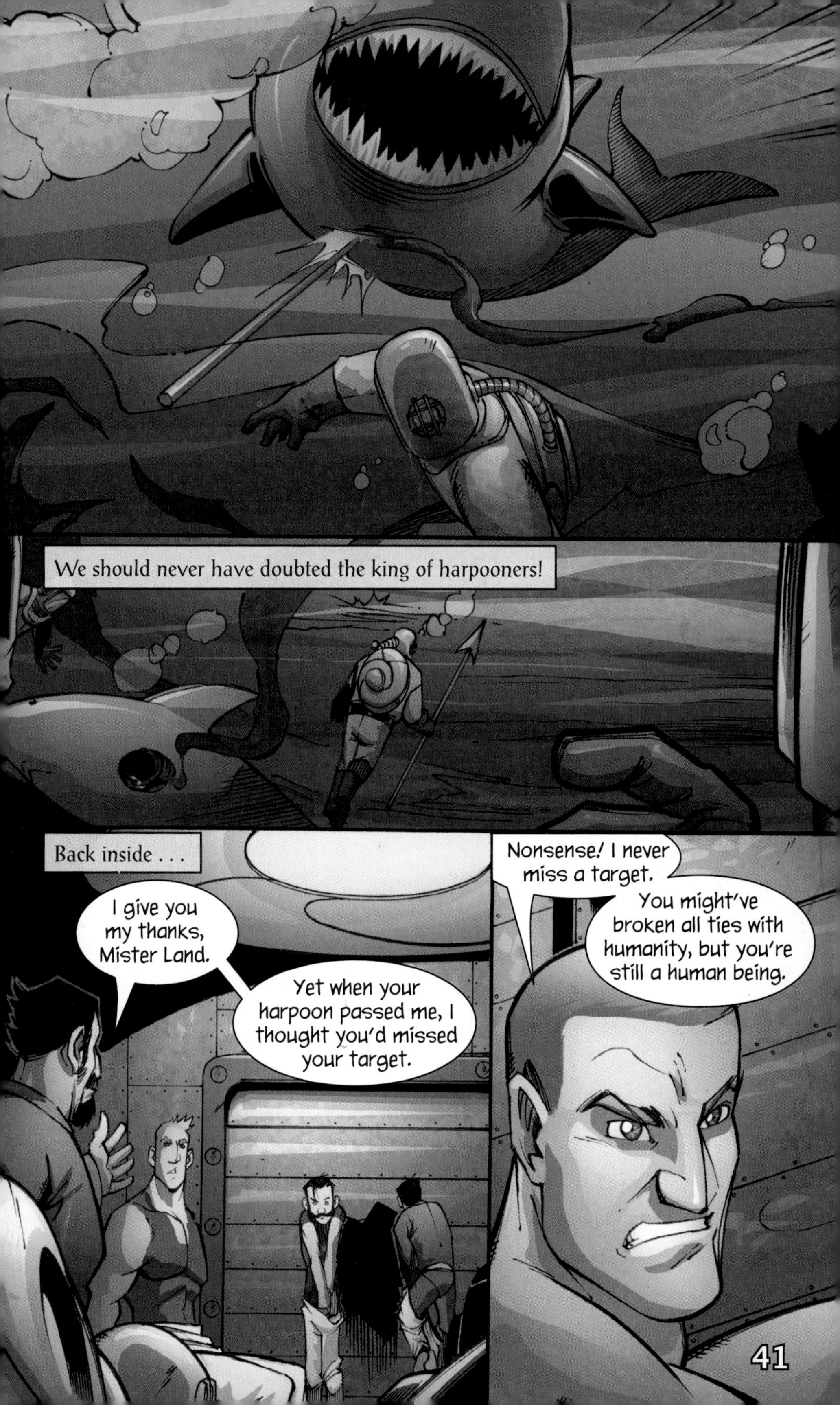

We should never have doubted the king of harpooners!
Back inside . . .
I give you my thanks, Mister Land.
Yet when your harpoon passed me, I thought you'd missed your target.
Nonsense! I never miss a target.
You might've broken all ties with humanity, but you're still a human being.

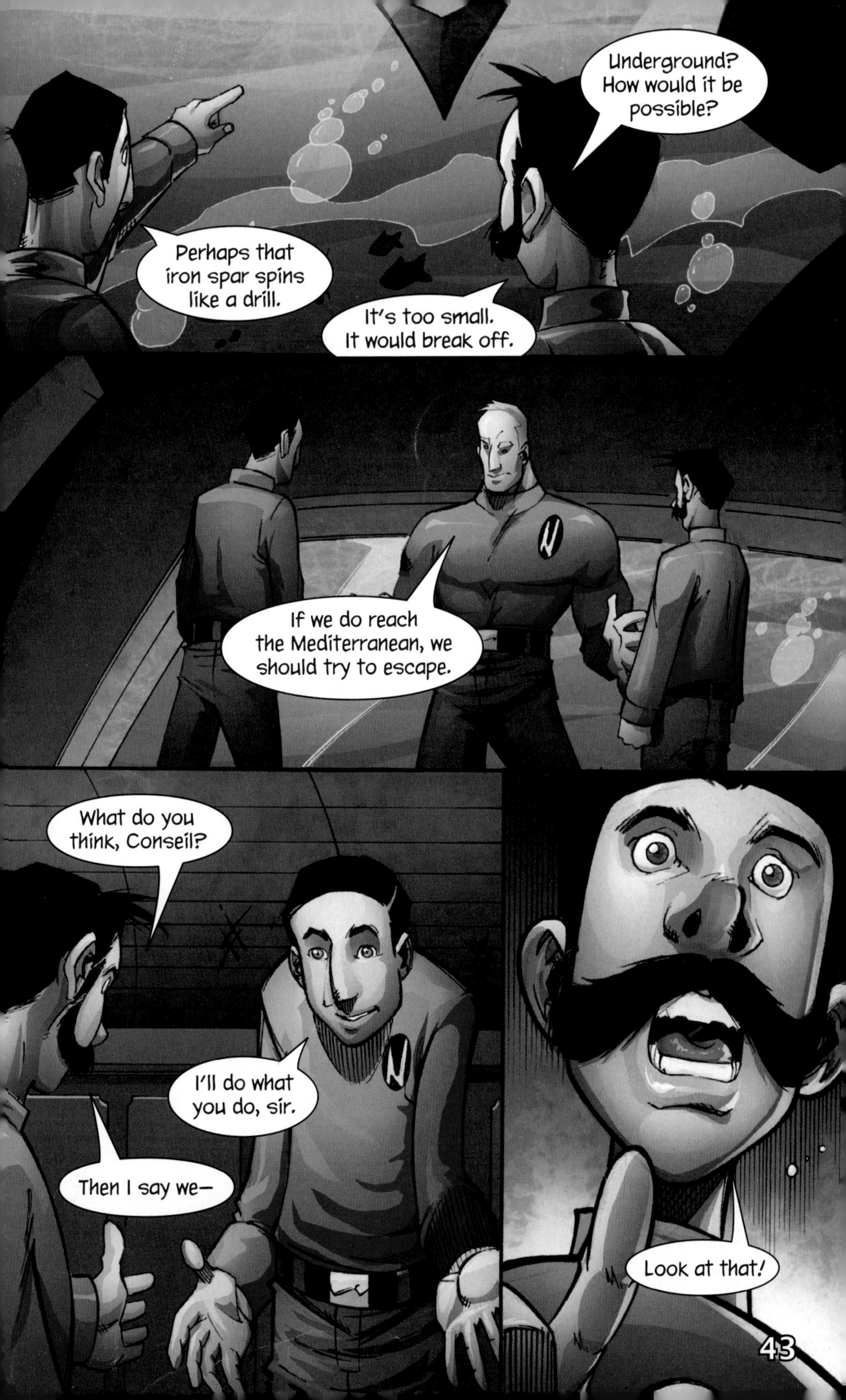
Underground? How would it be possible?
Perhaps that iron spar spins like a drill.
It's too small. It would break off.
If we do reach the Mediterranean, we should try to escape.
What do you think, Conseil?
I'll do what you do, sir.
Then I say we—
Look at that!

45

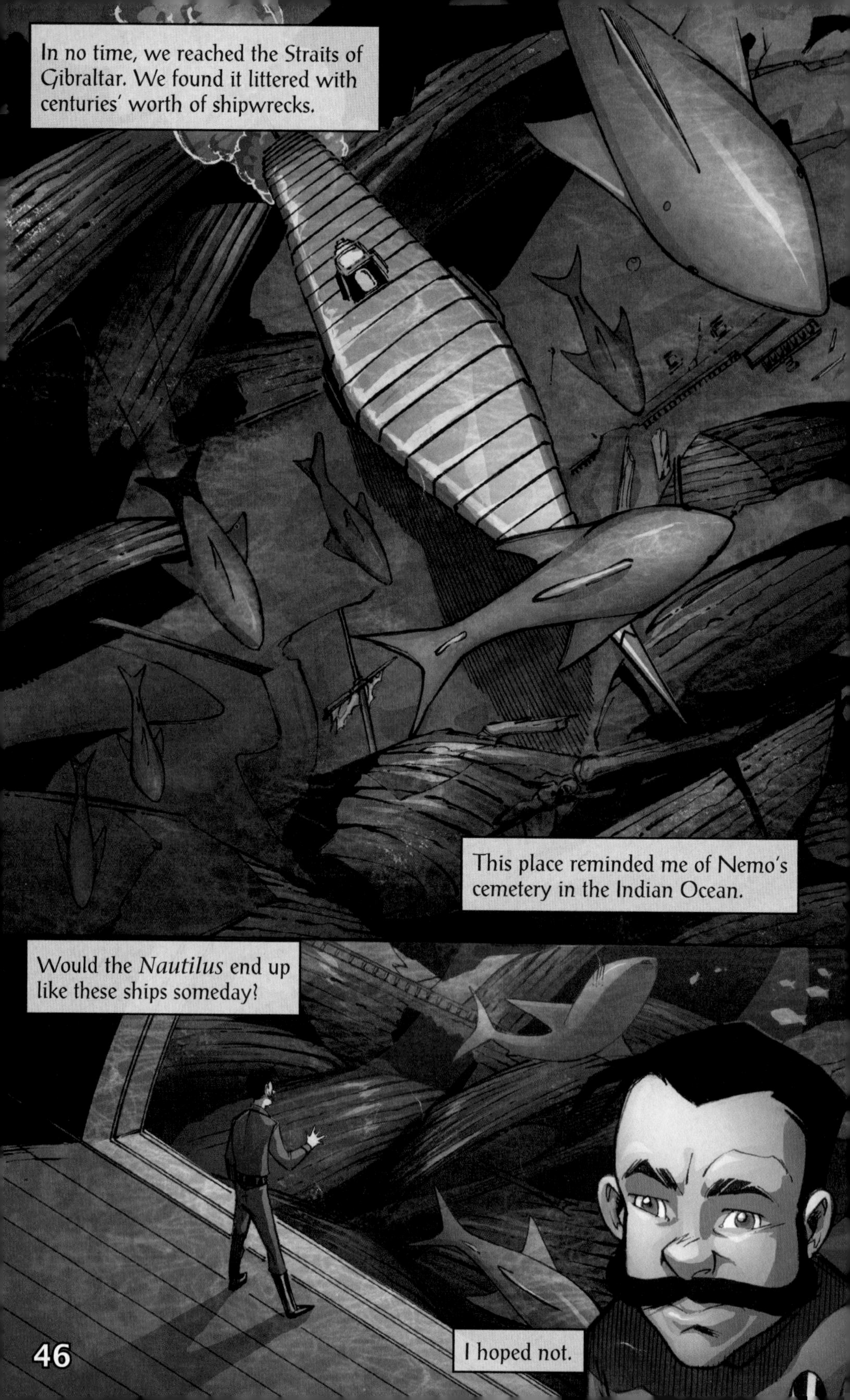
In no time, we reached the Straits of Gibraltar. We found it littered with centuries' worth of shipwrecks.
This place reminded me of Nemo's cemetery in the Indian Ocean.
Would the *Nautilus* end up like these ships someday?
I hoped not.

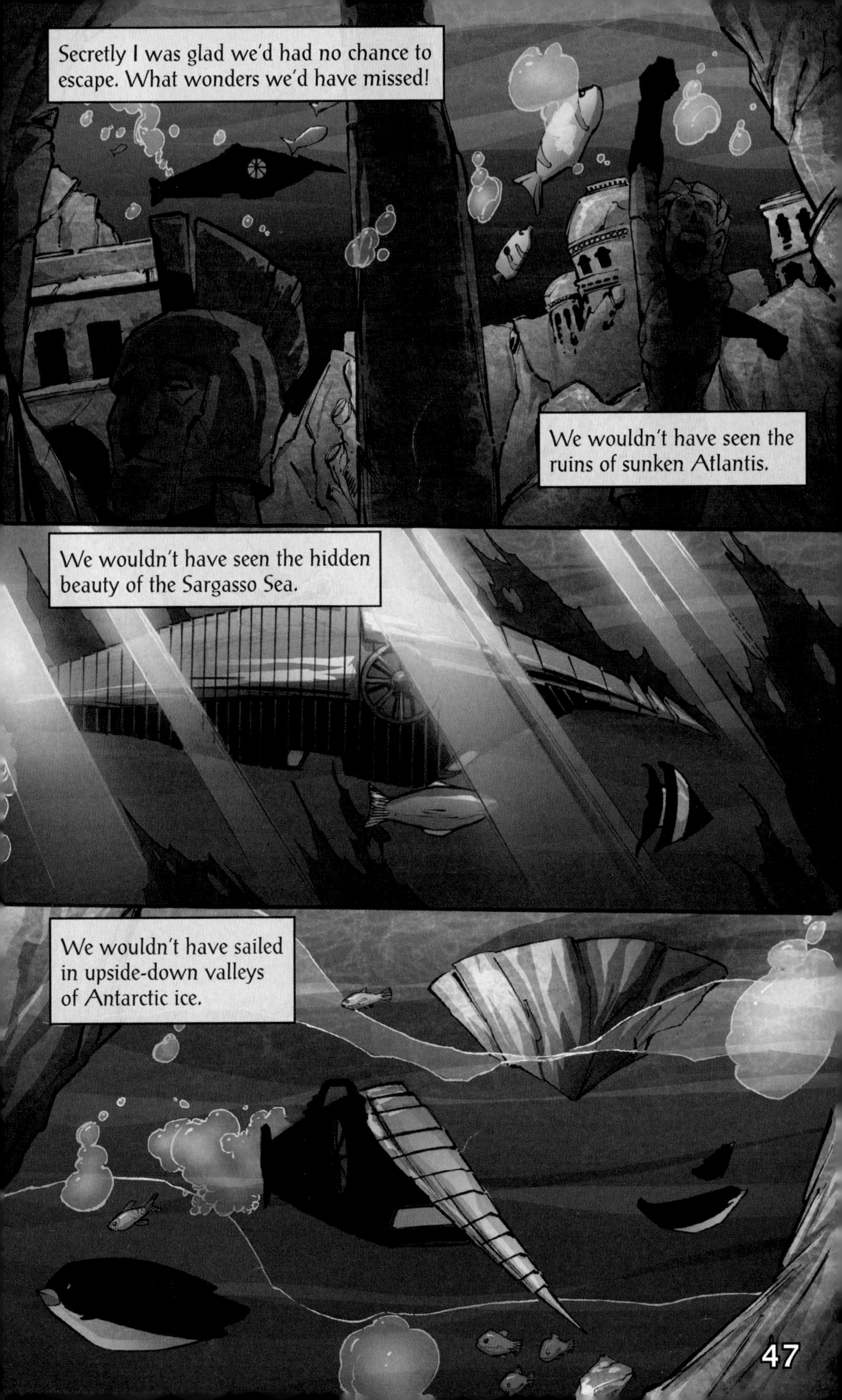
Secretly I was glad we'd had no chance to escape. What wonders we'd have missed!
We wouldn't have seen the ruins of sunken Atlantis.
We wouldn't have seen the hidden beauty of the Sargasso Sea.
We wouldn't have sailed in upside-down valleys of Antarctic ice.

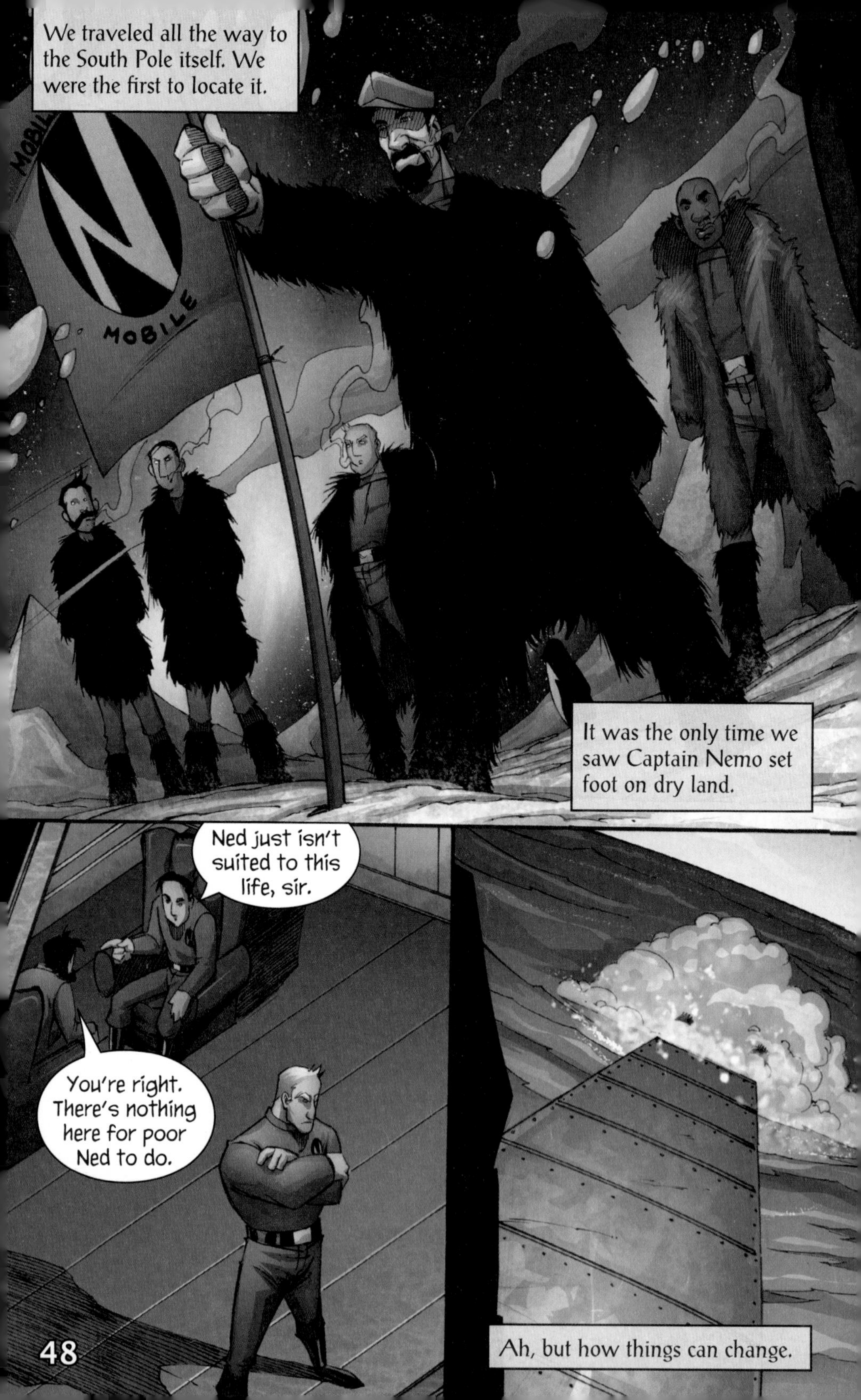
We traveled all the way to the South Pole itself. We were the first to locate it.
MOBILE
MOBILE
It was the only time we saw Captain Nemo set foot on dry land.
Ned just isn't suited to this life, sir.
You're right. There's nothing here for poor Ned to do.
Ah, but how things can change.

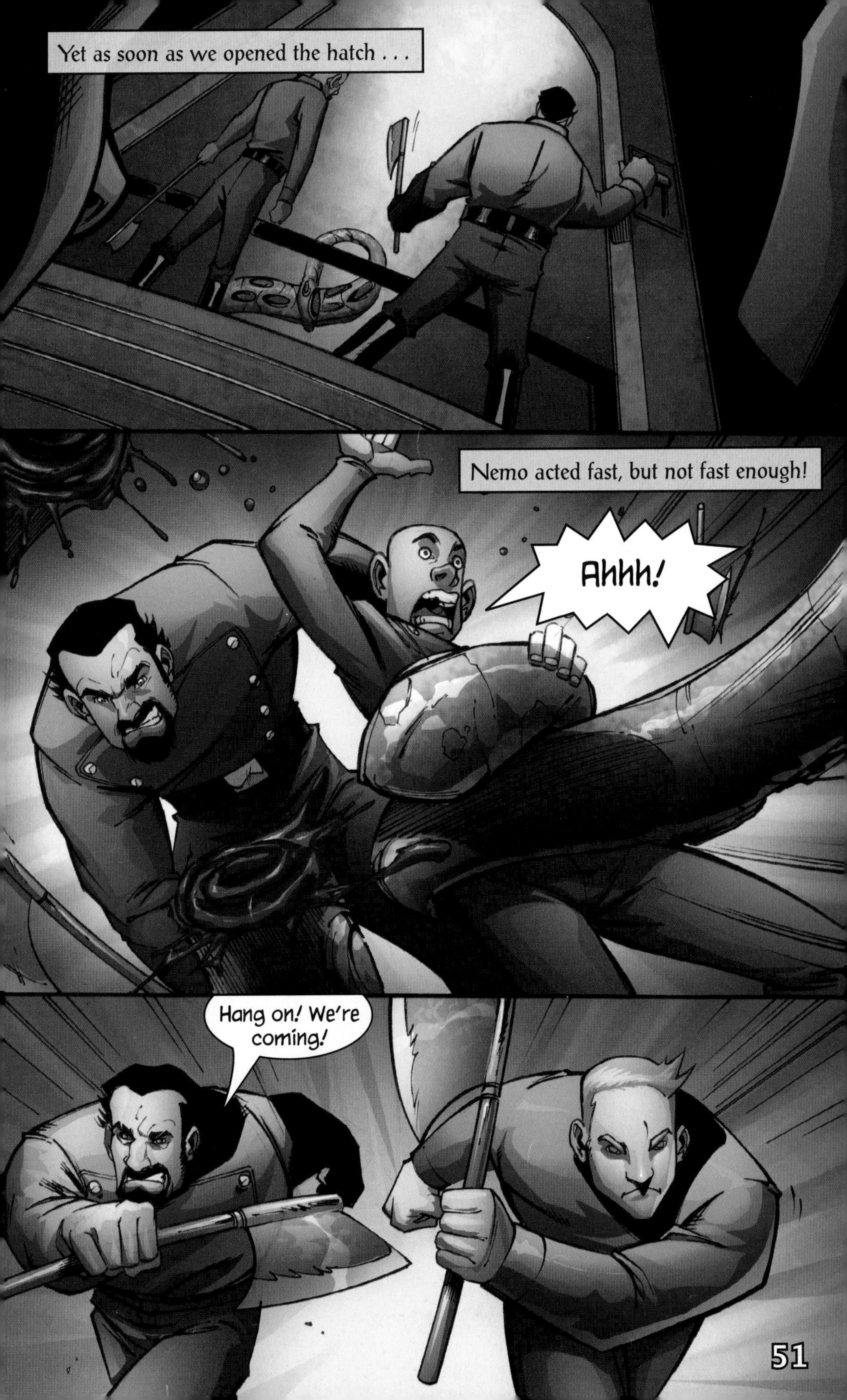
Yet as soon as we opened the hatch . . .
Nemo acted fast, but not fast enough!
Ahhh!
Hang on! We're coming!

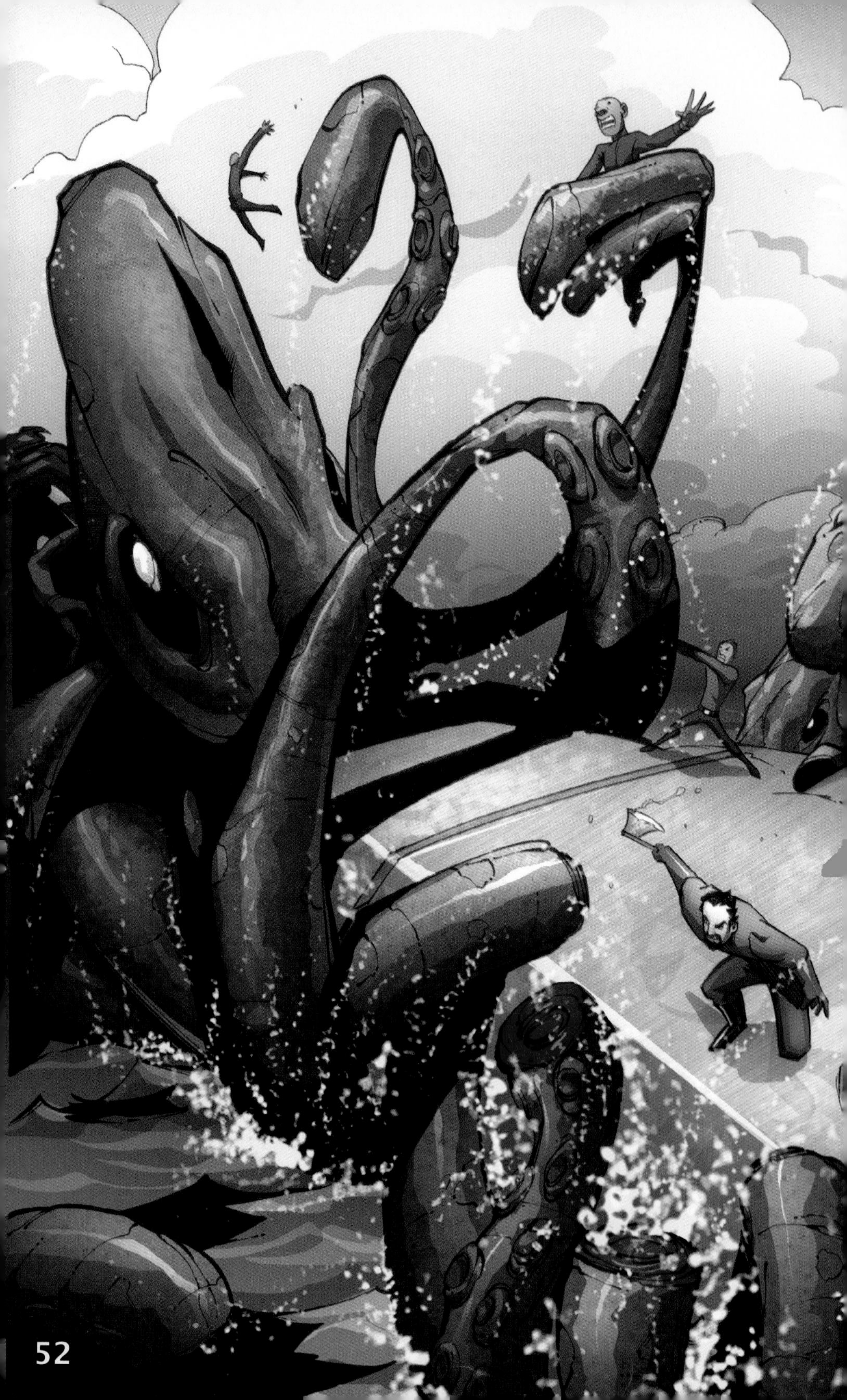

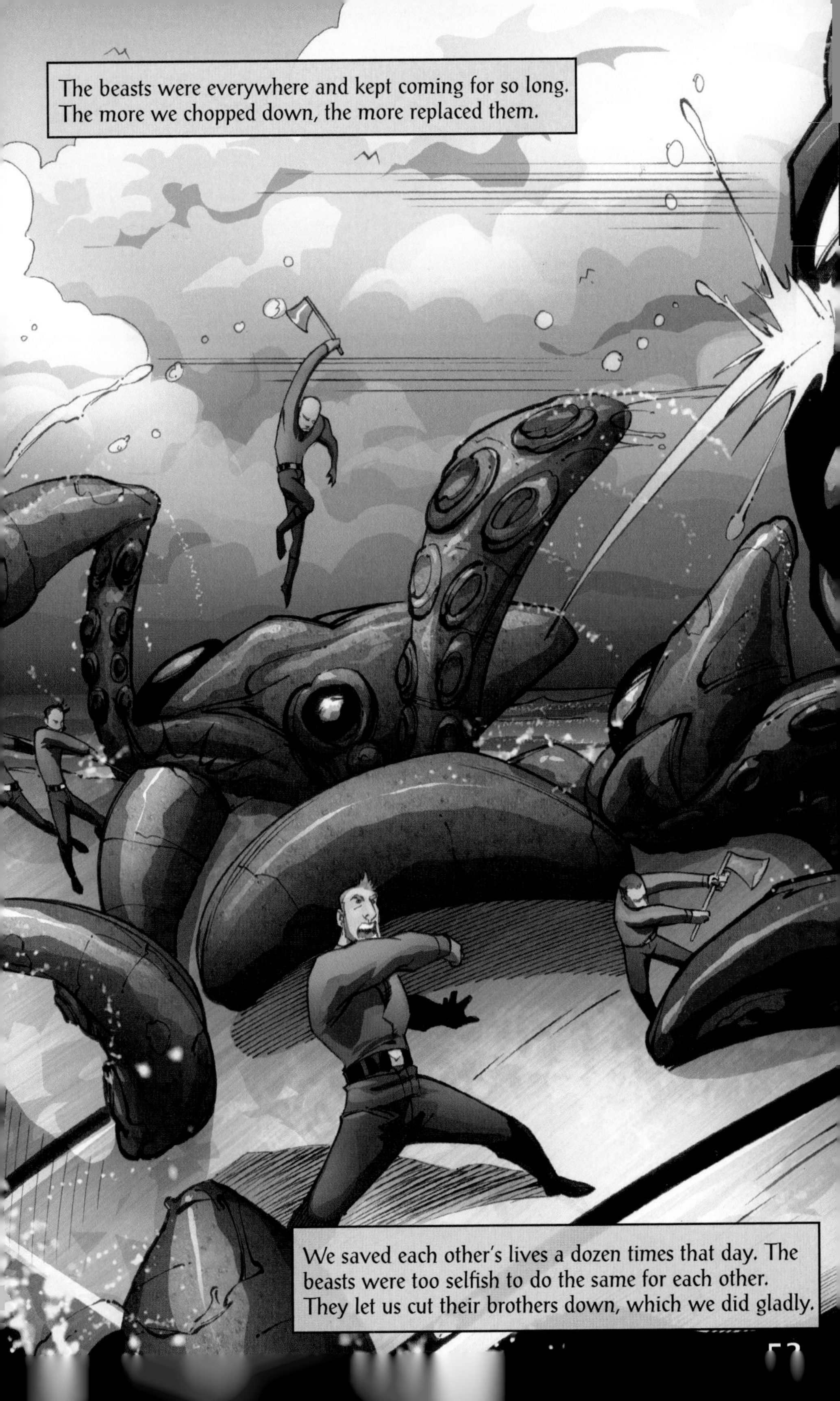
The beasts were everywhere and kept coming for so long. The more we chopped down, the more replaced them.
We saved each other's lives a dozen times that day. The beasts were too selfish to do the same for each other. They let us cut their brothers down, which we did gladly.

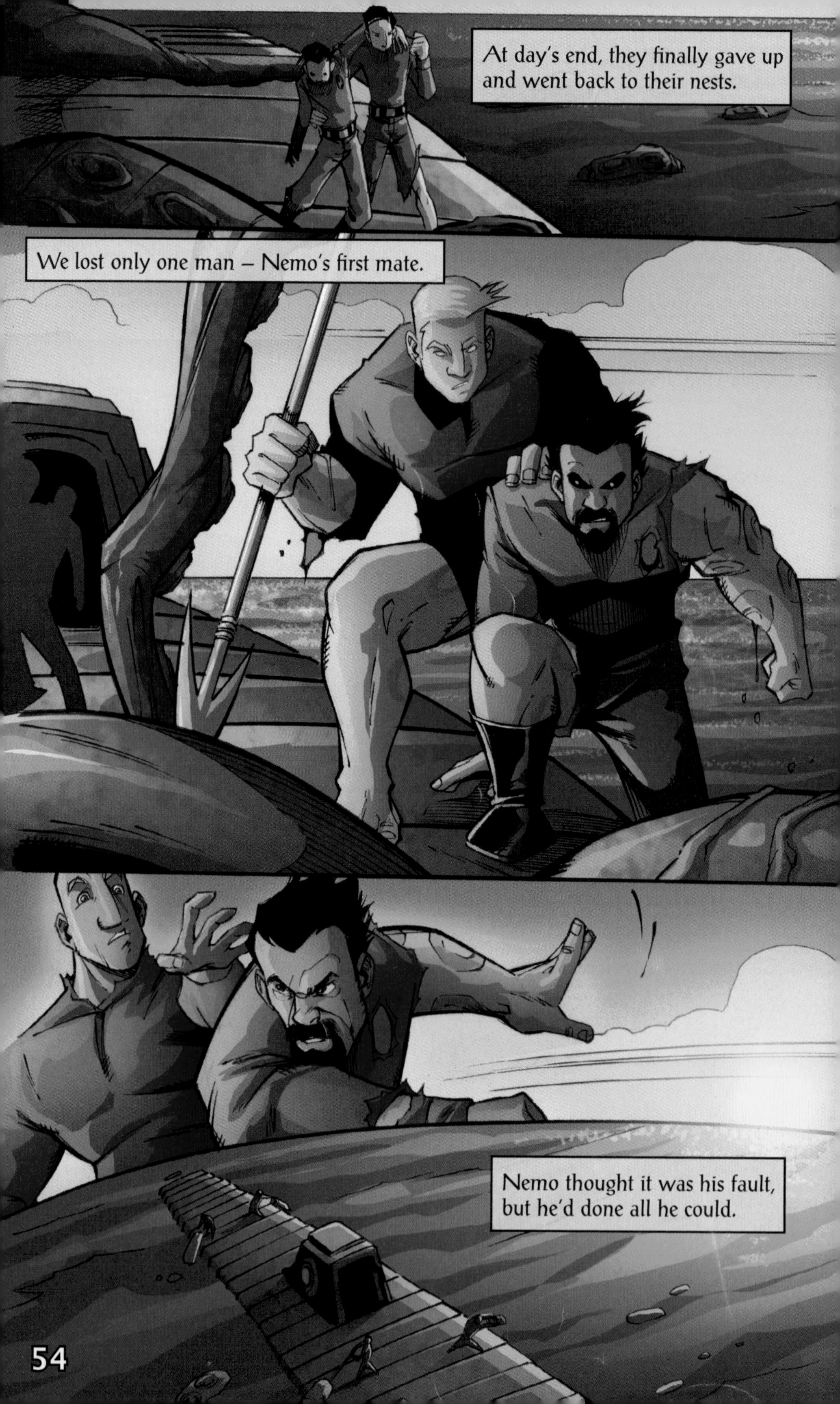
At day's end, they finally gave up and went back to their nests.
We lost only one man – Nemo's first mate.
Nemo thought it was his fault, but he'd done all he could.

Chapter 5: The Voyage Ends

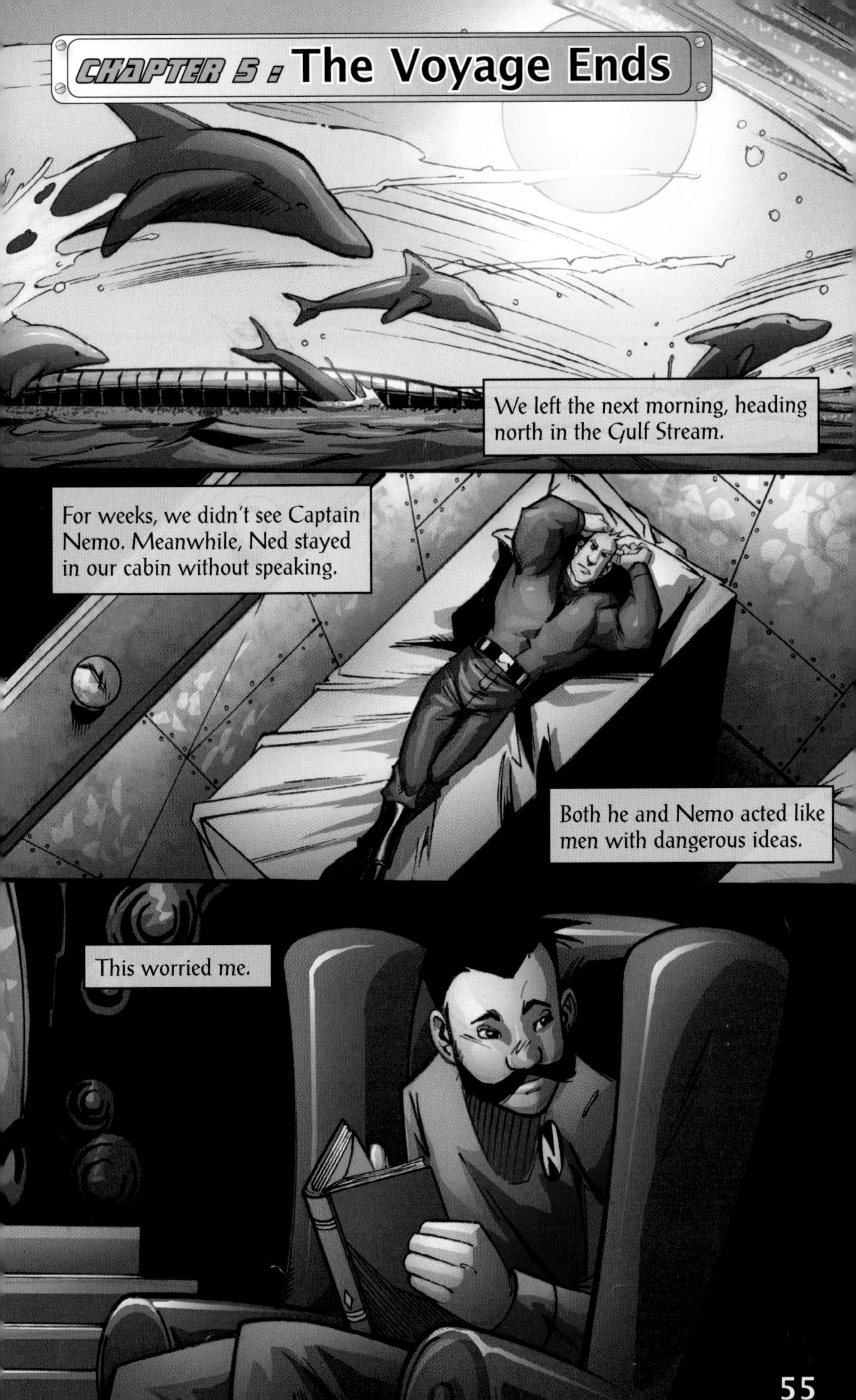
We left the next morning, heading north in the Gulf Stream.
For weeks, we didn't see Captain Nemo. Meanwhile, Ned stayed in our cabin without speaking.
Both he and Nemo acted like men with dangerous ideas.
This worried me.

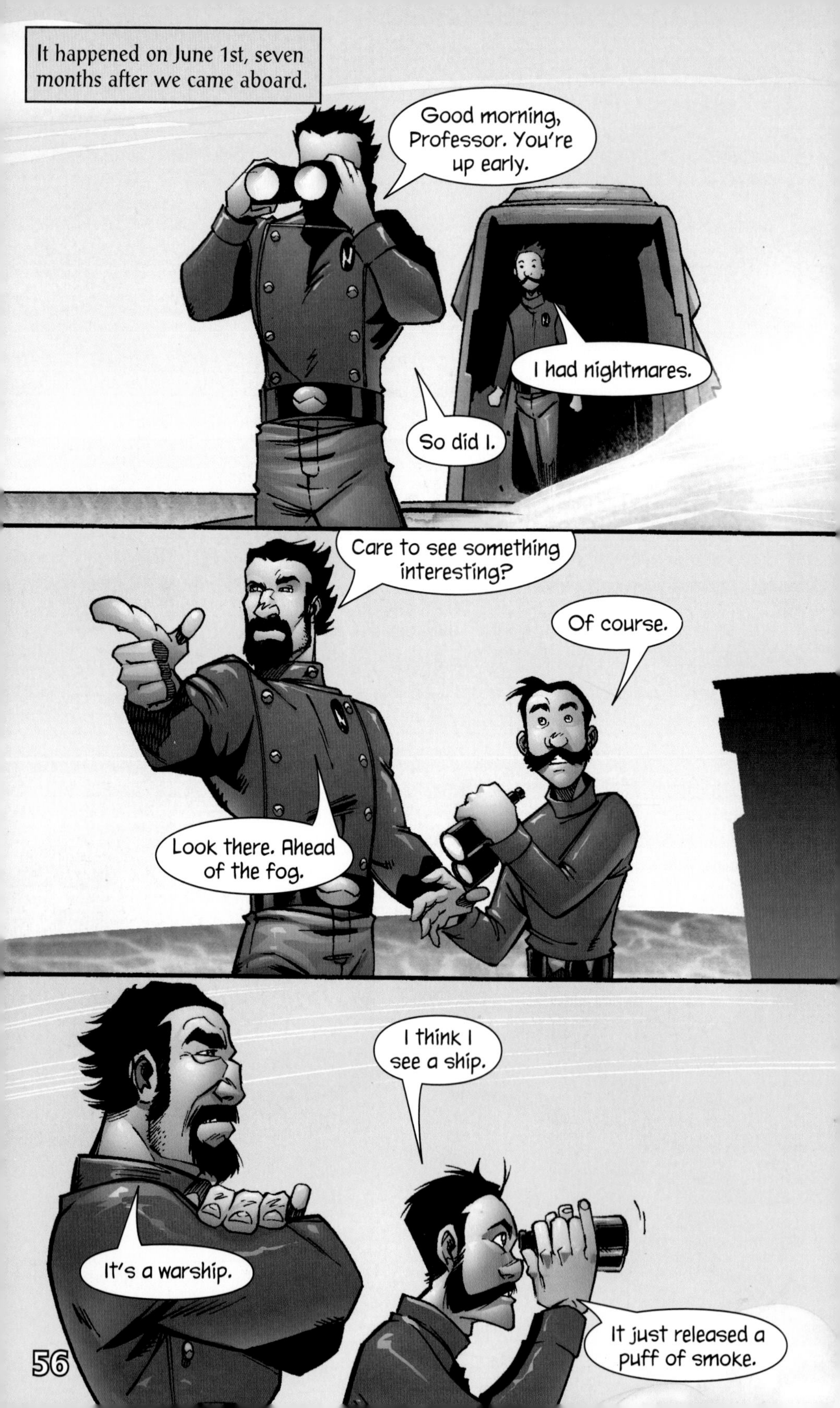
It happened on June 1st, seven months after we came aboard.
Good morning, Professor. You're up early.
I had nightmares.
So did I.
Care to see something interesting?
Of course.
Look there. Ahead of the fog.
I think I see a ship.
It's a warship.
It just released a puff of smoke.

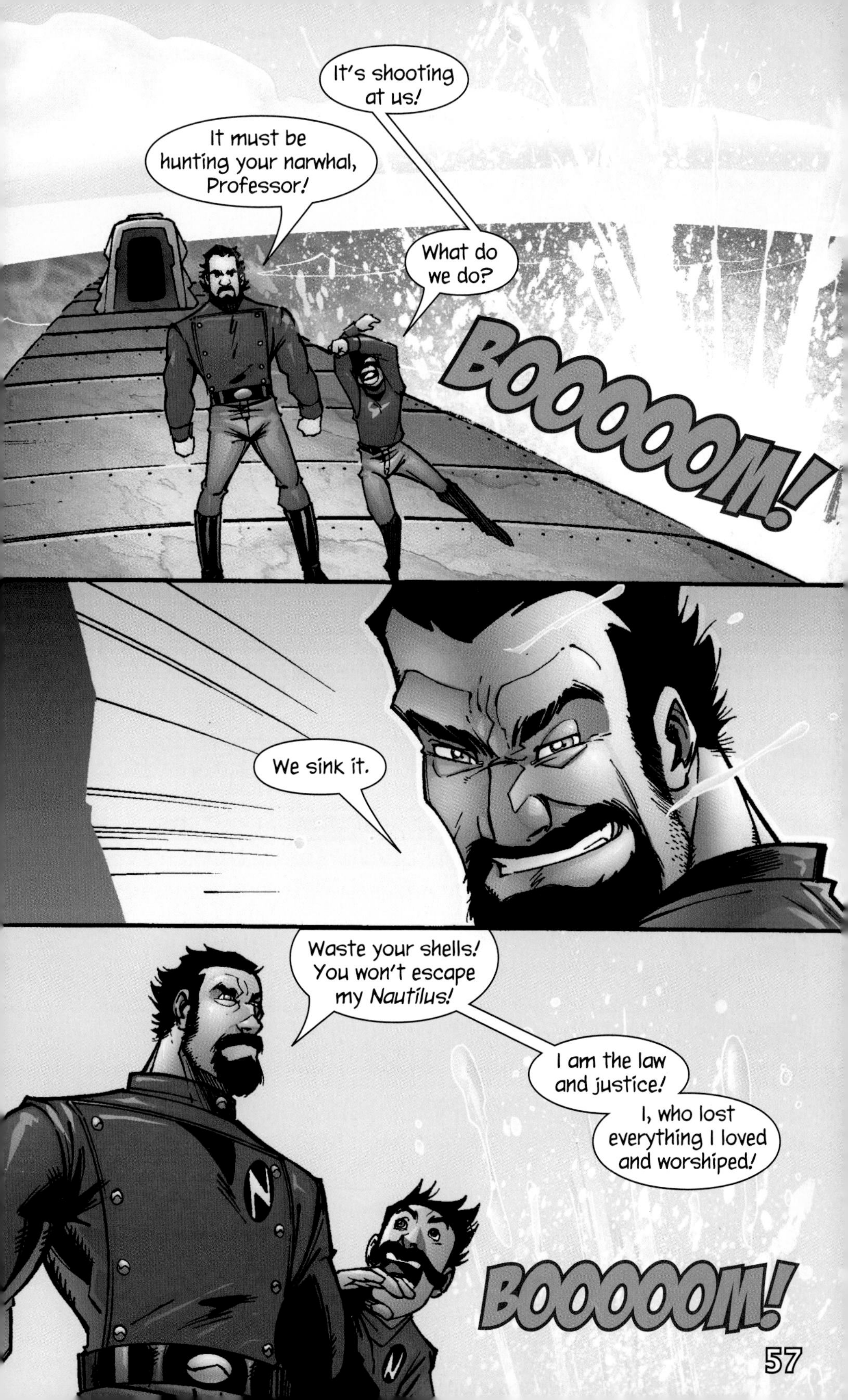
It's shooting at us!
It must be hunting your narwhal, Professor!
What do we do?
BOOOOOM!
We sink it.
Waste your shells! You won't escape my Nautilus!
I am the law and justice!
I, who lost everything I loved and worshiped!
BOOOOOM!

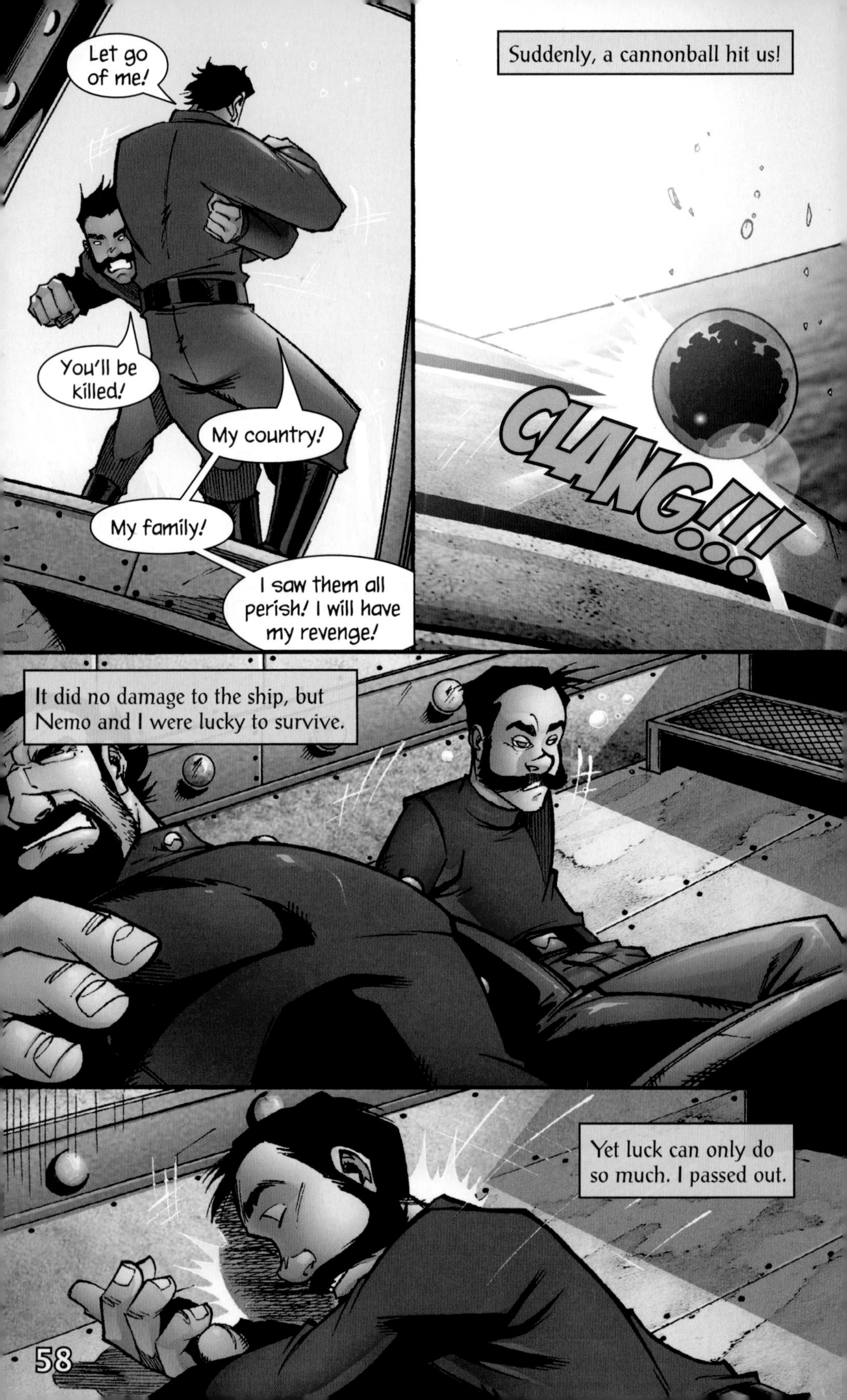
Let go of me!
You'll be killed!
My country!
My family!
I saw them all perish! I will have my revenge!
Suddenly, a cannonball hit us!
CLANG!!!
It did no damage to the ship, but Nemo and I were lucky to survive.
Yet luck can only do so much. I passed out.

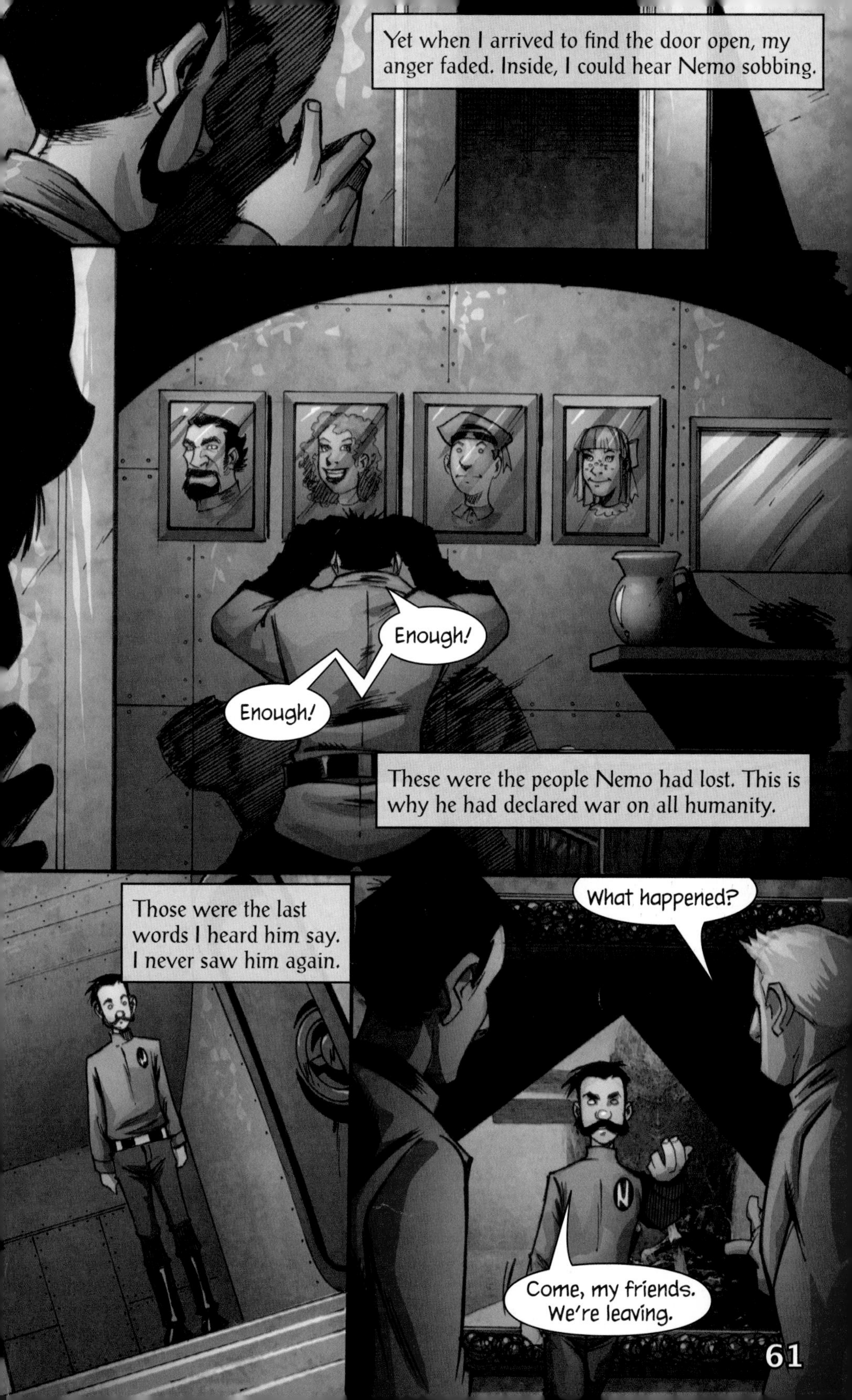
Yet when I arrived to find the door open, my anger faded. Inside, I could hear Nemo sobbing.
Enough!
Enough!
These were the people Nemo had lost. This is why he had declared war on all humanity.
Those were the last words I heard him say. I never saw him again.
What happened?
Come, my friends. We're leaving.

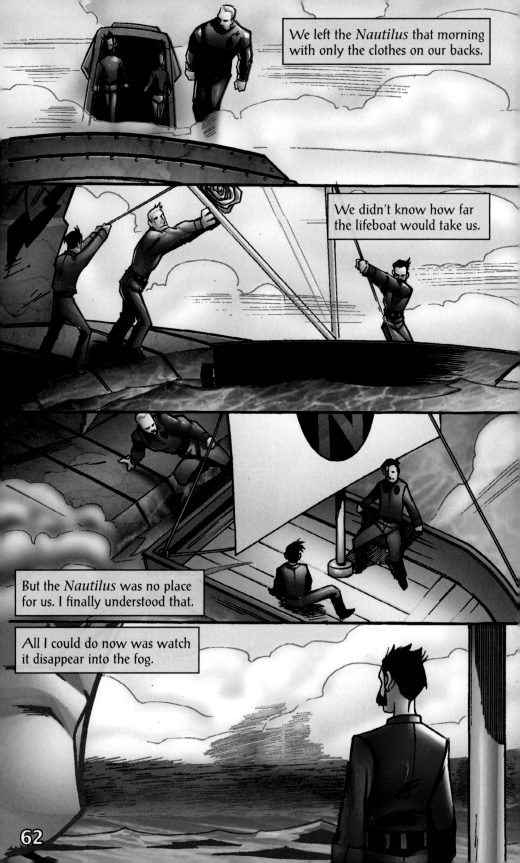

We left the *Nautilus* that morning with only the clothes on our backs.

We didn't know how far the lifeboat would take us.

But the *Nautilus* was no place for us. I finally understood that.

All I could do now was watch it disappear into the fog.

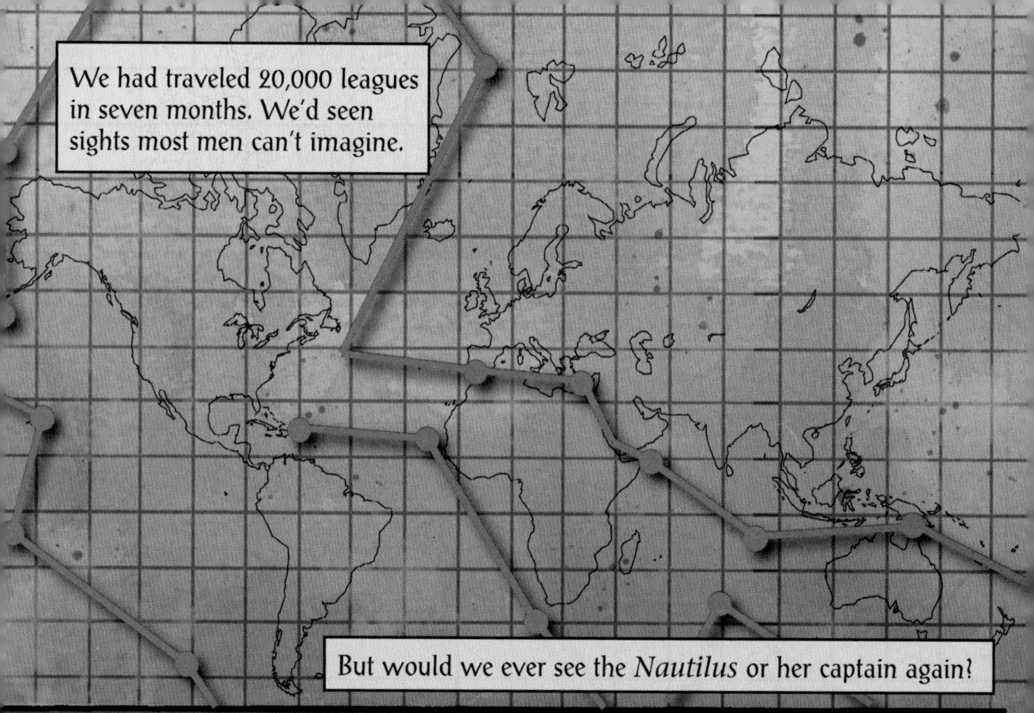
We had traveled 20,000 leagues in seven months. We'd seen sights most men can't imagine.
But would we ever see the *Nautilus* or her captain again?

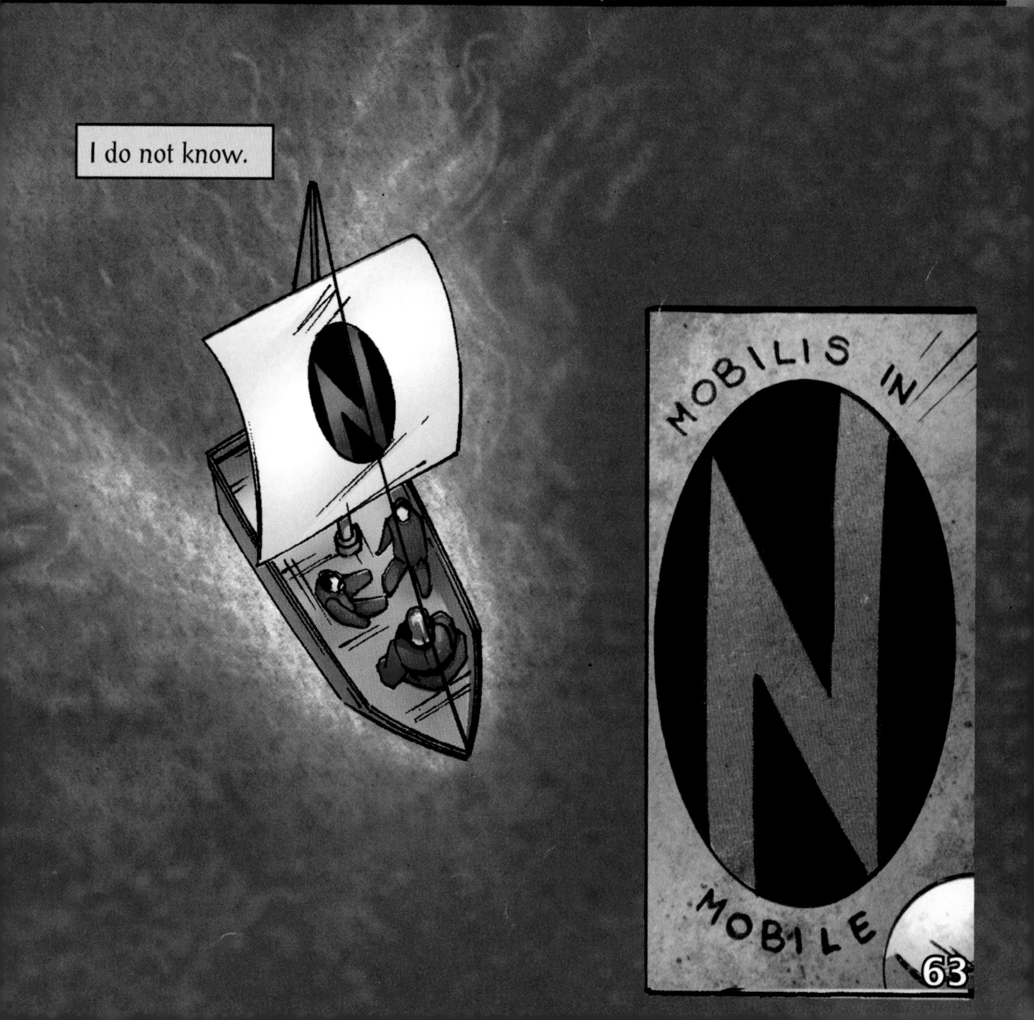
I do not know.
MOBILIS IN MOBILE

ABOUT THE AUTHOR

Jules Verne was born on February 8, 1828, in France. Growing up near a river, the constant sight of ships sparked his interest in travel. As a young man, Verne even tried to run away and become a cabin boy. Fortunately, his father caught him, and soon Verne was off to study law in Paris. While there, Verne escaped the boredom of his studies by writing stories. When his father found out about this hobby, he stopped sending money for school. Verne started selling his stories, many of which became popular, including *20,000 Leagues Under the Sea* in 1870. Before he died in 1905, the author bought a boat and sailed around Europe.

ABOUT THE RETELLING AUTHOR

Carl Bowen is a writer and editor who lives in Lawrenceville, Georgia. He was born in Louisiana, lived briefly in England and was raised in Georgia where he attended grammar school, high school, and college. He has published a handful of novels and more than a dozen short stories, all while working at White Wolf Publishing as an editor and advertising copywriter. His first graphic novel, published by Udon Entertainment, is called *Exalted*. This book, *20,000 Leagues Under the Sea*, is his first book for Stone Arch Books.

GLOSSARY

binoculars (buh-NOK-yuh-lurz)—an instrument people look through to make distant objects appear closer

canal (kuh-NAL)—a passageway that connects two bodies of water

chamber (CHAYM-bur)—a small room or closed-in space

civilized (SIV-i-lized)—having manners and an education

harpoon (har-POON)—a large spear often used to hunt fish or whales

humanity (hyoo-MAN-uh-tee)—all human beings

justice (JUHSS-tiss)—a judge or someone that enforces a set of rules or laws

league (LEEG)—a unit of measurement; one **league** equals about three miles (five kilometers).

lounge (LOUNJ)—a room where people can relax, such as a living room or lobby

mobilis in mobile (MOH-bee-leess IN MOH-bee-lay)—a Latin phrase meaning "moving through moving waters"

narwhal (NAHR-wol)—a whalelike, ocean animal about 20 feet long with long tusks

theory (THEER-ee)—an idea that explains the reason for something

DIVE DEEPER
INTO SUBMARINES

Many people believe Alexander the Great was the first person to journey underwater in a contained vessel. Legend says the Greek leader explored the Aegean Sea inside a glass barrel around 333 BC, more than 2,000 years ago.

Artist Leonardo Da Vinci, who painted the famous *Mona Lisa,* also worked on plans to build an underwater ship during the 1500s. However, Da Vinci kept his plans a secret because he feared the invention would be used for war.

Less than 300 years later, Da Vinci's prediction came true. David Bushnell built the first submarine used for battle. The *Turtle,* as it was called, was made of wood, held one person, and could stay under water for a half hour. On September 6, 1776, the American army used the *Turtle* against a British warship. The attack was unsuccessful.

During the Civil War, the United States Navy tested their first submarine. The *Alligator* measured 47 feet long and could hold more than 14 crew members. While being towed into battle in 1863, a storm sunk the sub off the North Carolina coast. It has never been found.

Early subs were often powered by oars or hand-cranked propellers. The United States Navy launched the first nuclear-powered submarine in 1954. It was named the *Nautilus,* the same as Captain Nemo's underwater vessel. In 1958, the *Nautilus* became the first sub to cross beneath the North Pole.

Nuclear energy has since powered some of the fastest subs ever built, including Russia's Alfa class submarines. These subs could travel nearly 300 miles per hour!

On January 23, 1960, *Trieste* became the deepest-diving underwater vessel ever built. The *Trieste* dove nearly 38,000 feet before reaching the floor of the Pacific Ocean.

DISCUSSION QUESTIONS

1. If you were trapped in Nemo's submarine, would you want
   to escape like Ned Land, or would you enjoy the ride?
   Explain your answer.

2. Ned Land didn't seem to trust Captain Nemo. So, why do
   you think he saved Nemo from the shark? Explain your
   answer using details from the story.

3. Do you think Captain Nemo will ever get over the people
   he has lost and return to the surface? Or, do you think he
   will spend the rest of his life at sea? Why?

WRITING PROMPTS

1. Write your own underwater adventure. What would your submarine look like? Where would you travel? What type of creatures would you face?

2. At the end of the story, the *Nautilus* submarine disappears into the fog. Where do you think it will go next? Write a story about another voyage with Nemo and his crew.

3. Imagine you were going on a year-long underwater voyage and could only pack three things. What three things would you take with you and why?

OTHER BOOKS

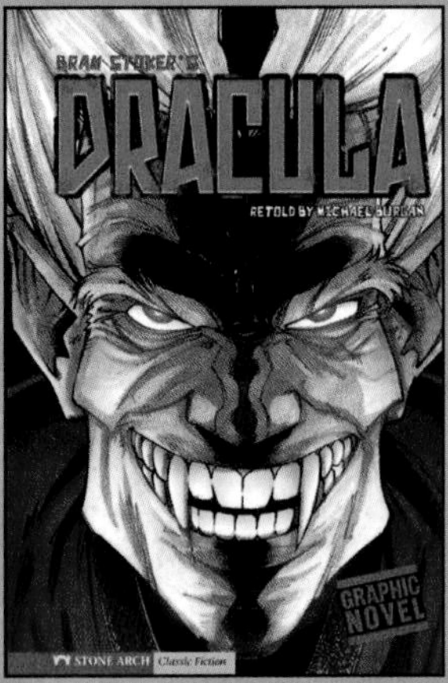
BRAM STOKER'S
DRACULA
GRAPHIC NOVEL
STONE ARCH
Classic Fiction

Dracula

On a business trip to Transylvania, Jonathan Harker stays at an eerie castle owned by a man named Count Dracula. When strange things start to happen, Harker investigates and finds the count sleeping in a coffin! Harker isn't safe, and when the count escapes to London, neither are his friends.

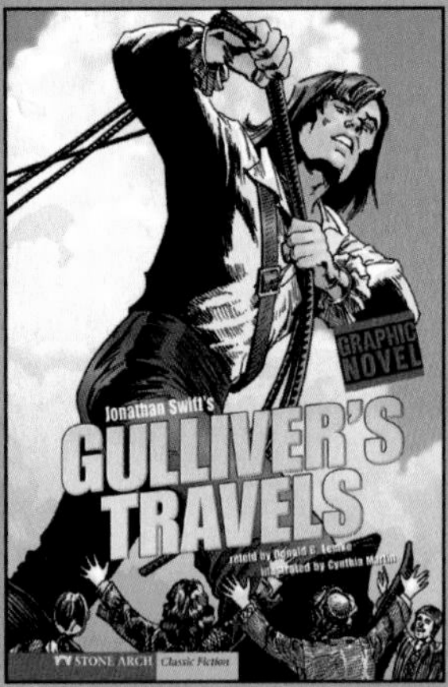
GRAPHIC NOVEL
Jonathan Swift's
GULLIVER'S TRAVELS
STONE ARCH
Classic Fiction

Gulliver's Travels

Lemuel Gulliver always dreamed of sailing across seas, but he never could have imagined the places his travels would take him. On the island of Lilliput, he is captured by tiny creatures no more than six inches tall. In a country of Blefuscu, he is nearly squashed by an army of giants. His adventures could be the greatest tales ever told, if he survives long enough to tell them.

THE LEGEND OF
SLEEPY HOLLOW
GRAPHIC NOVEL
STONE ARCH Classic Fiction

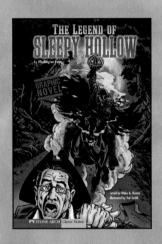

Sleepy Hollow

A headless horseman haunts Sleepy Hollow! At least that's the legend in the tiny village of Tarrytown. But scary stories won't stop the town's new schoolmaster, Ichabod Crane, from crossing through the Hollow, especially when the beautiful Katrina Balt lives on the other side. Will Ichabod win over his beloved or discover that the legend of Sleepy Hollow is actually true?

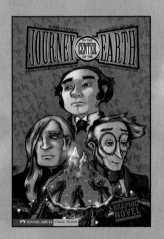

JOURNEY TO THE CENTER OF THE EARTH
GRAPHIC NOVEL
STONE ARCH Classic Fiction

Journey to the Center of the Earth

Axel Lidenbrock and his uncle find a mysterious message inside a 300-year-old book. The dusty note describes a secret passageway to the center of the earth! Soon they are descending deeper and deeper into the heart of a volcano. With their guide Hans, the men discover underground rivers, oceans, strange rock formations, and prehistoric monsters. They also run into danger, which threatens to trap them below the surface forever.

INTERNET SITES

Do you want to know more about subjects related to this book? Or are you interested in learning about other topics? Then check out FactHound, a fun, easy way to find Internet sites.

Our investigative staff has already sniffed out great sites for you!

Here's how to use FactHound:

1. Visit www.facthound.com

2. Select your grade level.

3. To learn more about subjects related to this book, type in the book's ISBN number: **9781434204479**.

4. Click the **Fetch It** button.

FactHound will fetch the best Internet sites for you!